◆ ◆

Tye spent his early years being taught all the means of survival by his father, Ben Watkins, who had been quite famous as a mountain man during the 'shining times'. Tye honed these skills over the years to earn the reputation as the best scout in the army.

He was now Chief of Scouts at Fort Clark, Texas, and on what he thought would be a simple assignment to locate an overdue pay wagon led him into many dangerous situations and bloody conflicts with Border bandits and a band of renegade Apaches.

◆ ◆

Border Trouble

◆◆

by

Gary McMillan

authorHOUSE™

1663 LIBERTY DRIVE, SUITE 200
BLOOMINGTON, INDIANA 47403
(800) 839-8640
WWW.AUTHORHOUSE.COM

This book is a work of fiction. People, places, events, and situations are the product of the author's imagination. Any resemblance to actual persons, living or dead, or historical events, is purely coincidental.

© 2005 Gary McMillan. All Rights Reserved.

No part of this book may be reproduced, stored in a retrieval system, or transmitted by any means without the written permission of the author.

First published by AuthorHouse 08/12/05

ISBN: 1-4208-5265-5 (sc)

Printed in the United States of America
Bloomington, Indiana

This book is printed on acid-free paper.

A special thank you to my mother-in-law Carolyn Emerson for her support and to my sister Sharon who never let me give up on my dream of being a published author.

I have not read a lot of westerns in my life, but in this case it did not matter. I found BORDER TROUBLE evocative. I found the lead character, Tye Watkins, not simply heroic but multi-dimensional. I found myself hooked by the plot and I was totally mesmerized by the quality of Gary's voice, deceptively simple yet haunting and in some places beautiful.

--Buzz Bissinger

◆ 1 ◆

Slumped in the saddle, Tye felt as if a huge fist had hit him in the stomach taking all the air out of him. He had lived here along the Border all his twenty nine years and had been fighting bandits and Apaches since he was fourteen. He thought he had seen the worse that a man could see but this was way beyond anything he had seen before. Ahead of him, a little ways off the Old Mail Road was the largest flock of buzzards he had ever seen. Under the mound of these revolting creatures, he could see blue pants with the yellow stripes of the cavalry. The buzzards were ripping the bodies apart with their long beaks, fighting over the strips of human flesh. Tye, recovering from the initial shock of the carnage, pulled his navy colt and fired two rounds at the birds. They expressed their displeasure at him as they scattered. They didn't go far, settling on some near by boulders waiting for this intruder to leave so they could get back to their feast.

Tye was upset with himself for firing the pistol. In this part of Texas, there were plenty of outlaws looking for some easy money and there were more than enough Apaches to go around also. For the most part a man was better off if no one knew he was around. Firing those shots let anyone within a mile or so know where he was. He led his horse toward the wagon to tie him to it as the sorrel was becoming nervous and skittish and hard to handle with the sight and smell of all the blood. The last thing he wanted was to get thrown and lose his mount. He was twenty miles from any town or fort and being on foot in July would be dangerous in the Texas heat. He forced his mount toward the wagon and at the same time studied the scene.

He noticed the men had been scalped and two had arrows in them. He also saw a lot of shod pony tracks as well as a lot of boot tracks. Very few Apaches rode ponies that were shod and none he had ever seen wore boots. He figured this was bandits trying to put the blame on the Apaches again... namely Tanza. Tanza was a fierce warrior who hated the white man with every fiber of his soul. He was leading a small band of warriors that had been raising hell on both sides of the Border. Tye also knew the Apaches had no need for money and the money box was gone from the wagon.

He started to dismount when a bullet burned his left shoulder and plowed into his horse's head. The horse reared and Tye threw himself to the side, away from the falling horse hitting the road bed hard, stunning him for a couple of seconds. He recovered, started to get up when two more bullets buzzed by like angry bees striking the road bed. He scrambled on his hands and knees toward the ditch beside the road throwing himself into it and rolling over on his back.

The fine alkali dust that covered the Old Mail Road lay like a thick blanket and after falling in it and bear crawling to the ditch, Tye's hands and clothes were covered by the white powder. He raised himself up slightly so he could see over the top of the shallow ditch. Three puffs of smoke followed by the reports of the rifles caused him to lie back down immediately. Bullets struck the top of the ditch throwing the alkali dust into the air and settling on him, getting into and burning his eyes and clogging up his nose making it difficult to breathe.

It wasn't midmorning yet and he was sweating profusely, partially from the heat and part from the exertion of the last few seconds. Tye knew he was in a tight. Lying in a ditch with no water and no hat under a July sun in Texas wasn't a pleasant way to spend a day. Then, there was the problem of someone trying to blow your head off every time you moved. He wished he had put the strap of his hat under his chin like it was designed for. His hat would help tremendously under this sun but it was lying on the road having come off when he hit the ground.

It was hot, and getting hotter by the minute and Tyes' old buckskin shirt was clinging to him like a second skin. It had been only about thirty minutes since he had thrown himself into the ditch but it seemed hours ago. He could feel his face burning and his mouth was so dry he couldn't spit if his life depended on it. He would probably laugh if he could see himself though. The white dust covered him and his face looked like a map with all the little trails his sweat made as it ran across his face.

Tye knew he had to get the shooters closer if he was going to have any kind of chance of getting out of this since all he had was his pistol and Bowie. At seventy or so yards his pistol was about as useful as a slingshot. But how? Plans came to him quickly but were dismissed just as quick. He peeked over the roadbed and looking at his dead horse renewed his vow to kill the bastards. Buck was the best horse he ever had and saved his tail more than once with his speed and endurance. He was way too good to end up like this... buzzard bait.

~

Two Bears, Tanza's little brother, and his two friends, White Owl and Two Moons had left the band earlier, determined to earn a little respect from the older warriors. Tanza had brought them along so they could see what it was like to be on a raiding party but they were not going to be involved other than being responsible for the horses. They knew stealing some horses or maybe killing and scalping one of the hated Pindah-lickoyees, or white eyes, would do this. They, as all young Apache boys their age, had been training since they could walk for one thing...to be a warrior and to live as their fathers had... free. Free to come and go as they please; to raid the hated Comanche for horses and take their women; raid the homesteads and kill the white eyes that were trying to force them off their land; to hunt and make babies. This was the way their fathers had lived and their father's father had lived.

The three young men wanted this respect more than anything. When they heard the shots fired by Tye, they were only a short distance away. They climbed the hill and when they looked over, saw Tye. They knew this was their chance to earn that respect. They would kill and scalp the man and take the fine looking horse he was riding. They had missed with their first shots and regretted they had killed such a fine looking horse but now were going to take their time in killing this hated white man. They knew he wasn't going anywhere.

~

"This is a hell of a way to die." Tye said disgustingly. "Trapped in a ditch and if I don't get out, I'll be looking like a piece of over done bacon. The worse part is not knowing who has me trapped." It came to him of a sudden. This happened to his pa when he and Bridger were trapping in the Yellowstone in the '30's. Pa was in this same pickle as Tye, except it was two Blackfoot warriors. Pa had told the story to him twenty years ago. He was trapped and decided to draw their fire and pretend to be hit and play dead. When the Blackfoot warriors came to scalp him he shot one with his pistol and killed the other with his knife. Tye could now do the same thing and only hoped to have to fake being hit. But first he shut his eyes, relaxed and thought for a moment about yesterday and the events that led him to be in this fix.

♦ II ♦

"Major Thurston," the orderly said saluting." Mr. Watson is here as you requested.

"Good, show him in, Corporal," Thurston said.

The Corporal saluted again, back straight as an arrow, then did an about face and marched stiffly out.

'Army needs to spend more time teaching these men to ride and shoot than all that protocol crap,' Tye thought to himself.

"Howdy, Major," Tye said jovially and immediately knew this wasn't gonna be a social visit.

Thurston, instead of offering him the usual cigar had turned his back to him and walked to the window, standing there looking out, hands clasped behind his back. He stood there for a full minute while Tye was trying his hardest to figure out what he had done, or not done, that had him in trouble.

"What did I do to upset you Major?" Tye hesitantly asked.

Thurston slowly turned around and looked at Tye, "You haven't done anything, Tye. I just believe we have a big problem right now and I.....".He was interrupted by Tye.

"Wouldn't be the overdue pay wagon would it, Major?"

Thurston exploded, "How in the hell do you know about the pay wagon?" he demanded.

Tye, startled for a second at the outburst, said. "I don't know Major. I guess it's common knowledge around the Fort. I heard it somewhere but paid it no never mind. The stinking pay wagon is never on time anyway. We haven't seen one for almost two months."

Thurston startled Tye again by slapping his desktop with the palm of his hand, scattering papers and then dejectedly, sat down in his chair. He leaned forward and put his elbows on the desktop and his head in the palm of his hands and quietly said.

"This damn army can never keep anything quiet. Tye, this was a big payroll and only a few select people supposedly knew about it."

"How big?' Tye asked.

"Two months' pay. This month and one month back pay for the troops at Ft Duncan, Camp Verde, and here at Clark. Pay for about four hundred men altogether. If you figure an average of about twenty dollars per man per month, that's roughly sixteen thousand dollars."

Tye let out a low whistle, "That's a lot of money coming at one time. I can see why you'd be worried, Major, but I think they probably had some trouble like an axel or wheel busting."

"Yeah, I thought of that but the Old Mail Road is in awful good shape and I can't see the wagon busting anything. I've always trusted my gut feelings and right now it's telling me that something has happened and it's not a breakdown."

"What could happen?" Tye asked. "With that much money there's gonna be a sizeable escort. I know we have several gangs running around this part of Texas, but none that would tackle a large cavalry escort."

"I can't believe that everyone in the Fort knew it. I just can't figure how in hell's name word got out," Thurston said, shaking his head.

"You know, Tye, it's not easy being assigned out here in the middle of nowhere. These men need that money so they can go into town and do whatever to let off some steam. No pay this time means more than two months since the last time they were paid. We've got to find that pay wagon and get it here or we are going to start having morale problems, desertions, and a hell of a lot of fights among the men."

Tye now knew why he had been summoned to Thurston. "When do I leave Major?"

"If the wagon doesn't come in tonight, I would like to see you leaving before sunup in the morning. I've already signed this requisition," he said as he handed it to Tye. "Go to the quartermaster and get what you need."

Tye, taking the requisition, started to leave but looked at Thurston and asked, "There was a large escort wasn't there Major?"

Thurston sighed and said ,"No, there were four."

Tye laughed and then saw that the Major was serious. "You're not kidding me are you?"

"I wish I was but the thinking, if you can call it that, was that a large escort would draw too much attention and a small one leaving at three o'clock in the morning, would not be noticed. Only a handful of key people knew the time and details."

Tye was quiet for a few seconds then let go, "What in hell's name are those stupid asses in San Antonio thinking. Do they believe this country is as frigging safe as the street that they and their fat assed wives live on there in the city. Hell, we have a dozen damn bands of outlaws running around out here including that stinking Alex and Frank Vasquez and their band of cutthroats. If that ain't enough, you have the Apache, Tanza, and his band of renegades.

"I know all that Tye, I'm as upset as you are about this," Thurston said.

"The hell you are," Tye said emphatically, then added, "I bet they have a snotty nosed Second Lieutenant that has never even heard a shot fired except on the stinking rifle range leading it."

"You're pretty much right Tye," Thurston mumbled as he collapsed back in his chair. "There is an escort of four, plus the paymaster and a civilian driver."

"So let me get this straight, Major. We have a $16,000 payroll which would tempt any gang, an escort of only four, and a secret departure that everyone in the State of Texas knew about." Tye said summing things up. "God, this army is screwed up'" he uttered shaking his head in disbelief as he left.

Thurston walked over to the window and looked out at the parade ground where he saw and heard First Sgt O'Malley screaming and cursing at some green recruits. He was proud of his first command here at Clark. He loved the army life but he understood Tye's feelings. He had seen some pretty stupid things done by men in authority and this one was close to the top of his list. He just couldn't express himself as Tye had. In spite of the situation he smiled, thinking of the way Tye had so colorfully described his feelings.

He had a goal as Commander of Fort Clark. He fully intended to add his name to the list of Post Commanders that had done so much for this part of the country. Commanders like LaMotte who had built the fort in '52 and like Wilcox, who with the 4th Cavalry, regarrisoned the Fort after the Civil War in December of '66 and was Thurston's predecessor. These men had been firm in their resolution to make this wild and wonderful country safe for people to settle in and make a life for themselves. This was his goal also and anything or anyone be damned if they tried to deter him from accomplishing it.

~

Tye picked up his supplies from the quartermaster and headed to O'Malley's quarters to see Rebecca. She was O'Malley's niece and had been living with them since her parents were killed about six months ago. Tye thought, and he was not alone in this thinking, that she was the most beautiful woman in the world. She was taller than most and her dark brown hair, when not put up, reached below her waist. She was only nineteen years old but was mature way beyond her years. They had been courting for about two months and was the first item on the gossip list when the women got together at a social, or a quilting party. As they would say, it's a match made in heaven, what with the Fort's most eligible bachelor and the prettiest girl seeing each other.

Tye could not believe his good fortune of having Rebecca as his girl. She made him feel different when she was around than he had ever felt with other girls he had known... not that he had known many. There wasn't an abundance of single girls out here except for the ladies at the saloons. He didn't know for sure, but he thought he was maybe falling in love, which in itself is not strange, but in Tye's case it was. He had never loved anyone except his parents...and his horses so he wasn't sure what this feeling meant. He had always spread the word that he would never get married and settle down and was proud of his bachelorhood. He didn't know it yet but the trap was already baited -- Rebecca was hopelessly in love with him.

"Tye Watkins," her voice startled him as he approached the porch. "What in the world are you doing here at this time of day?"

"Just thought I'd drop by to see you before I left."

"Left, what do you mean? Where are you going?"

"Orders, probably be leaving first thing in the morning."

"What orders? I thought you would be here for Saturday's Fourth Of July Celebration,"

"You're full of questions aren't you," he stated. "How about, hi Tye, sure glad to see you or something to that affect."

She was silent for a moment then said, "Hi Tye, sure glad to see you'" and she reached up and put her arms around his neck and pulled his face down to give him a long kiss.

"Now, is that better?" she asked as she pecked him on the cheek.

"Much more to my liken than all those rapid fire questions'. He said.

They stood looking in each other's eyes for a long moment before she said, "I'm still waiting for an answer."

"Persistent little girl, aren't you" he said laughing.

She stepped back, crossed her arms across her breast and stood there, tapping her foot.

"The pay wagon and its escort is way overdue and the Major has asked me to leave in the morning to look for it if it doesn't arrive tonight."

"Do you think something dreadful has happened?" she asked.

"Naw, probably a broke wheel or busted axel," he said not wanting to worry her none. It worked because she relaxed. The small talk about the weather, other couples, and holding each other close took the place of the questions.

"Do you know some of the men have gotten up a money pot on whether you and I get married or not?" she said hoping to get a hint of how strongly he felt about her.

"Which way is most of the money going?" he asked.

"I don't know the answer to that," she laughed, but inside she had her hopes up.

They visited for a few more minutes, making more small talk and holding hands before he said he needed to get some things done before leaving in the morning.

"I shouldn't be gone but for a day or so. I'll be back in time for the celebration."

They stood on the porch and melted into each others arms, holding tight to each other like there would be no tomorrow. He gave her one more kiss and was gone.

~

His thoughts of Rebecca ended as a shadow crossed his face. Opening his eyes he could see buzzards circling above him, getting lower and lower as he watched. " I ain't ready to be your damn meal yet" he hollered.

The sudden noise startled the buzzards and flapping their huge wings, rose higher into the sky. They were still circling though, waiting patiently. He figured if he looked close he could see the miserable creatures licking their beaks. It had been almost a hour now and the heat was getting unbearable. He wasn't sweating as much as he was and he knew that wasn't a good sign.

"Ole son, if you are going to do something it needs to be quick cause in this heat you ain't going to be thinking too clear in about another hour, two at the most."

~

The sounds of the first shots got Alex Vasquez's attention. He stood up and walked a ways trying to figure what direction they had come from. It was hard to tell with him being in a canyon as he was. There were too many shots to be a hunter. He was still standing, listening, when the second round of shots came, and then a third. He was sure now that they were coming from the direction of the Old Mail Road, where they had left the dead troopers late yesterday. His gang didn't go far after the ambush and robbery of the pay wagon. They had this hidden canyon that they were sure no one except maybe the Apaches knew about. It was only a short ride from the road. They had drank all their tequila last night in celebration of their new found riches and all of his men were sleeping off the effects of it.

Alex walked over to where his brother, Frank was sleeping.

"Frank," he said while nudging him with the toe of his boot, "Frank wake up," he repeated.

Frank mumbled something incoherent and rolled the other way.

Alex kicked him in the butt, hard this time, "Frank get your lazy butt up, NOW," he shouted.

Frank raised up and rubbing his red, blood shot eyes looked up at Alex.

"Dammit Alex, what in the hell do you want?" he asked.

"I heard some shots being fired from over toward the Mail Road. I want you to go see what is going on."

Frank, cocking his head from side to side said "I don't hear no shots now. Maybe it was your imagination Alex. Maybe it was all the tequila you drank last night that made you think you heard shots."

Alex grabbed a handful of Frank's collar and shaking him said, "You get your lazy butt up now and take a couple of men and go see what the hell is going on."

Frank slowly stood up, swayed slightly, stretched and scratched himself before walking over to where Miguel and Jesus were passed out. He kicked the hell out of both of them a couple of times before they were roused from their slumber. Neither of them were in no mood for anything or anyone... except Alex. They weren't going to cross him drunk or sober. They listened to Alex's instructions and the three of them staggered to the horses. Alex was laughing at their attempts to saddle their mounts. When they finally did, as they were riding off, Alex could hear them muttering oaths under their breaths.

"One thing for sure, it won't take them long to sober up under this sun," Alex thought to himself, his broad shoulders shaking with his laughter..

He walked back to his bedroll in the shade of one of the two giant oak trees that were around the spring. The canyon was a perfect hideout. The narrow entrance was covered by mesquite and was only wide enough for one horse and rider at a time. The walls were vertical and curved inward at the rim. They were probably seventy-five feet high. The canyon was only about two hundred yards long and maybe fifty yards at the most in width. The spring and trees were in the back where it was only twenty yards wide. The spring formed a pool that was maybe three feet deep and the overflow ran toward the entrance in a small stream and then like so many other springs in this country disappeared into the ground, probably reappearing somewhere else. They had used this place many times and felt secure here.

Frank was the oldest of the two. Alex, however, was the clear leader of this bunch of cutthroats. He was the "boss" for several reasons, the least not being the fact he was the toughest and the most vicious of the lot. He was also cunning as a fox. He was always a step ahead of the Federales in Mexico and the Rangers in Texas. He didn't know it yet, but after messing with the army's payroll, he was fixing to have more than he bargained for after him. He was more curious than worried about the gunfire. He thought he had made the pay wagon ambush look like the Indians had done it.

"They won't be looking for whites or us Mexicans, but old Tanza had better watch his backside, " he said laughing.

~

It was time for Tye to get this thing over with. "Lord I haven't bothered you much by asking for help before but I could use a little now if it isn't no problem to you." Tye took a deep breath and rolled to his right again and looked over the road bed to the crest of the hill only to see smoke from the shooters rifles. He got a glimpse of black hair and red head bands. He rolled back immediately as bullets splattered around him. He grunted loudly, thrashed about for a few seconds, and then lay perfectly still as more of the white dust settled on him.

"Of all the rotten luck, it had to be Apaches." He thought to himself." No way that stupid stunt will work with them. There ain't nothing in the world more patient than an Apache. That was a stupid waste of."....... he stopped to listen to what sounded like rocks tumbling down the hill. He listened closely and heard the rocks again. They were coming, and he couldn't believe it. He knew the time to live or die was close at hand and for some strange reason he was impossibly calm and relaxed. Seems at times like this he was always relaxed, thinking. He figured this ability came from his pa. He flexed his fingers on his right hand to make sure he could handle the pistol. He heard the guttural sound of Apache talk and knew they were close, real close. He knew there were at least three and he hoped there were no more than that but it didn't make any difference-he was a dead man if he just lay where he was.. It was now or never. He gathered himself, jumped up screaming as loud as he possibly could, pulling his pistol at the same time. The youngsters, startled by this man jumping up, screaming, and looking like a ghost with all the alkali dust on him, took a couple of seconds to react. The two seconds was costly, as Tye fired at the first brave striking him square in the chest. The force of the bullet at this close range knocked him backwards into the brave behind him and both tumbled into the ditch on the opposite side of the road. Tye swung his gun hand to the right slightly and pulled the trigger again just as the third brave was raising his rifle. His hurried shot struck the brave in the shoulder spinning him around. Out of the corner of his eye he saw the brave that had been knocked down by the first he had shot raising his rifle to fire. Tye dove back into the ditch just as the bullet whistled by his head. He hit, rolled and raised his gun to fire again only to get a glimpse of the wounded brave being pulled down into the ditch by the one that just missed him.

"You did good Tye," he said to himself. "Now, instead of them being a hundred yards away, they are now only thirty or forty feet."

He did realize in his quick look that they were only boys. That was the only reason his little stunt worked. Seasoned warriors would have never fell for that. They were all in the same fix now. Neither he nor the Apache boys could move without chancing getting their heads shot off. He felt bad that he had killed a kid that couldn't have been more than fifteen or sixteen years old. The others looked the same age, but dammit, they were trying to kill him so he had no choice. A trigger sure didn't know the age of the person pulling it.

Frank Vasquez had climbed the hill behind where Tye was and reaching the crest looked over just as the three Apaches started down the hill. He watched the scene unfold and was impressed with this gringo. He also understood the problem that both, the white man and the Apaches now faced. Neither could move without getting shot. He slowly and quietly made his way back down the hill where Jesus and Miguel waited. He explained what had happened and the situation as it was now.

"This is what I want you two to do," he said. " Go about a quarter of a mile back up the road and cross over. Stay behind the hills and come up behind the hill where the Apaches are. Their horses should be tethered at the base of the hill you need to climb. Climb it and at my signal start shooting at the Apaches."

"Why we help this gringo?" Jesus asked.

"Stupid, we will kill the Apaches and take their scalps to sell and then we rob the gringo." Frank explained in an agitated voice.

This brought a laugh from each of them and they patted Frank on the back as they left. The two walked their horses a good distance before mounting to keep from alerting anyone to their presence. Frank had given them twenty minutes to get into position. He checked his watch and sat down in the only shade he could find, under his horse.

Frank had not been in favor of the army payroll job. He didn't want to get the army after them and he told Alex that. They had enough problems just staying ahead of the Rangers and the Federales. As usual, Alex had won the argument convincing him that his plan would put the blame on the Apaches, probably Tanza and his band. Besides, the amount of money involved was worth the risk. His contact in San Antonio had gotten word to him about the payroll, time of departure, and the small detail guarding it. It would be easy, and it had been. Frank checked his watch again and waited.

~

Tanza and his band were resting in the shade of a cliff. His braves were passing around a gourd of tiswin to each other. The tiswin was not as good as the white man's whiskey but the end result was the same. He was not taking any of it as his thoughts were on other matters. His little brother and his friends had been gone for a long time. He knew their desire to do something to gain them some status among the older warriors and he was afraid they had gotten themselves into trouble with their inexperience. They were all only fifteen summers old and had never been in battle. He walked to the edge of the shade, away from the others. He could see his beloved mountains in the distance, shrouded in a blue haze. His father and his father's father had roamed those mountains as well as the land where he now stood, as free men, to go and come as they wished. They lived as an Apache warrior should live, hunting and raiding. This was all they knew and what their grandfather's had known. This was the Apache way. All had changed with the coming of the white man. They wanted the land to own and the Apaches were in the way.

His grandfather's words spoken long ago to him came back now as if they were spoken yesterday instead of when he was a young man. "This land I live on, I love. The Great Spirit gave me legs to walk on it; eyes to see it's wonders and a head with which to think...it is said I am a enemy of the whites but I could live in peace...but they lie, steal, and take our lands." Those words were more true now than ever before. Tanza had listened to the white man once and moved to a reservation where he and his people were starving and not even allowed to hunt. He would never listen to the white man again and vowed he would kill them every chance he got.

"Is my friend worried about Two Bears?" Lone Wolf asked as he came up behind Tanza.

"You know me well, my friend," Tanza answered. "I'm afraid they may be in trouble."

"I have been thinking the same," Lone Wolf answered. "I will get some of the others and look for them."

"Look at them," Tanza said raising a clinched fist. "Already the tiswin has them in its clutches. They would be of no use. You and I will find them together." They mounted their ponies and with Lone Wolf, the better tracker of the two, leading, followed the tracks left by the three young warriors.

~

Frank checked his watch, got up from under his horse and after dusting his pants off, started up the hill, carefully and quietly. Extra care had to be taken because of all the loose rocks. When he reached the top, he carefully peered over. He could see the back of the gringo plainly but could not see the Apaches, but he knew where they were. Looking across the road to the opposite hill he saw Miguel and Jesus waiting for his signal. He sighted his rifle to where he knew the Apaches were and gave the signal and waited for what he knew was going to happen.

As soon as the two opened up, the Apaches raised up to return the fire and when they did, Frank shot one, then the other, right between the shoulder blades, the bullets exploding out their chest, splashing blood all over the rocks. Both were dead before they hit the ground.

It took Tye a second or two to realize the shots were not coming in his direction, and that some were even coming from behind him. Looking back and up he saw the grinning and waving Mexican. He looked across the road and saw two more coming down from that hill.

"What the hell," he exclaimed. "Where did they come from?"

Rising from the ditch, he walked swiftly to the wagon where the water barrel was. He could find out in a minute who they were but right now he needed water. Taking the cup he rinsed out his mouth and then poured two or three cups over this head, washing his face. He then took a long drink of the sweetest water he had ever tasted. The Mexican that had been behind him was approaching and Tye walked to him and shook his hand vigorously.

"I think you may have been in trouble, Senor." the Mexican said.

"You got that right. I was in big trouble," Tye said as he turned to shake the other two Mexicans hands.

From behind he heard the one Mexican say. "Senor, I think you still in big trouble."

Tye turned back toward him, "What do yo....".he never finished as a thousand lights went off behind his eyes and then all went black as he crumbled to the ground.

"Damn, Jesus, I think you killed him with that rifle butt." Frank said laughing.

Miguel kneeled down and felt of the side of Tye's neck. "Naw, he's still breathing but when he wakes up he's going to have one hell of a headache," he said, bringing more laughter from the others.

"You two take what you can off him and then get the Apache horses while I scalp these youngsters." Frank said.

Miguel flinched each time he heard the sucking sound as the scalps came off. They retrieved their horses as well as the Apache ponies, and rode back toward the secret canyon.

♦ III ♦

The sun was beginning to slip behind the hills when Tye opened his eyes. He started to raise himself up but became dizzy and nauseous and lay his head back on the ground. He felt of the bump on the side of his head. It was large and crusted over with dried blood. He waited a minute and again slowly raised himself up to a sitting position and sat there for a couple of minutes, trying to get his thoughts together. He stood up shakily, closed his eyes for a minute trying to stop everything from spinning. He opened his eyes and started walking slowly toward the wagon and the water barrel. He washed the blood off and wet his kerchief and wrapped it around his head. He drank his fill and immediately started feeling better. He looked at the dead Apaches and again felt the twinge of sorrow because of their age.

"You're a hell of a scout ole boy. You got yourself ambushed and near killed by three kids."

He shook his head in amazement. "Just damn kids."

He knew he needed to get away pretty quick cause someone was going to be looking for these three. He sure didn't want to be there to greet them. He started walking back toward Fort Clark when he saw the tracks... a horse with a notched shoe. He filed that in his memory for later. Walking away he looked back and said.

"Those three Mexican bastards will pay for this if it takes me the rest of my life."

~

"Corporal Johns," Thurston shouted from his office. "Would you check the duty roster and see who is on patrol in the morning and bring him to me." "Yes Sir" Johns answered from the adjoining office.

Thurston, sitting in his chair, leaned back, staring at the ceiling for a moment, then closed his eyes. It had been a long day. He was there when Tye had left before daylight and was still here as the sun was going down.

"Its been a long day and will be a longer night." he thought to himself. "No way it will be the longest though" as his mind went back to a night a few months ago. That was the first night he was alone after his wife had left to go back east. He had loved her as much as anyone could love anyone, and he still did, probably always would. There would never be another like her. They were happy the first year of their marriage. She was happy being the wife of a much in demand war hero after the Civil War. Parties and more parties were the order of the day in Washington. Being the daughter of a wealthy businessman she was used to the social life. Thurston was a soldier and was not crazy about that type of life. He applied for a command on the western frontier even though he could have had a cushy job somewhere in the East. When he received his orders assigning him to Fort Clark on the Texas frontier, he was elated. His wife and her mother cried for three days.

"This is the most Godforsaken country on earth." She exclaimed looking out the window of the army ambulance that had been dispatched form Fort Clark to San Antonio to bring Major Thurston and her to the Fort.

"Nothing but sand, rocks, and cactus, and those big ugly green bushes that I guess pass as trees out here."

"Those are mesquite, dear, and this land is covered with them. " Thurston said.

"I don't care what they are called, they are the ugliest things' I have ever seen."

Thurston saw where this conversation was headed so rather than get in a argument he kept quiet and let her rant and rave. Her tune changed forty eight hours later when they arrived at Fort Clark. Built around Los Moras Springs and Los Moras Creek, the land was covered in long grass, trees, and flowers.

"It's like a oasis in the desert," she said.

It wasn't enough to keep her happy long. With no stores to shop, no restaurants to dine in, and certainly no social life except the boring wives at a quilting party, she had had enough.

"I've tried so hard to like it here but I just am not cut out for this life." she said trying to hold back the tears.

"Can't you give it a little longer, honey," Thurston begged.

"NO," she said emphatically. I'm leaving on the next stage out and that's final."

She was gone within a week and with her, a part of Thurston.

◆ IV ◆

A knock on his office door jolted Thurston back to the present. "Yes." He said loud enough to be heard through the door.

"Lieutenant Garrison is here as you requested Sir. He is the officer scheduled for patrol in the morning." the Corporal answered.

"Good. Send him in."

The Corporal opened the door and Lieutenant Garrison entered the office. He stopped just inside the door and, standing at attention, gave a picture perfect salute. "Lieutenant Garrison reporting as requested, Sir." He said putting emphasis on the sir.

He held the salute while waiting for Thurston to return it. Thurston looked up slowly and returned Garrisons salute. He stood up and reached across the desk and shook Garrison's hand. He sat back down and was shuffling papers in a folder. "Don't stand there like a statue, Lieutenant, take a seat."

"Yes Sir." Garrison sat down on the edge of the seat, back straight and hands on his thighs.

Thurston looked up and smiled. He remembered the time he was on his first assignment and was summoned to the Post Commanders office for the first time. He was scared stiff. "First thing we need to do Lieutenant, is to remove that pole that is running up your butt and through your spine. Just sit back and relax so we can talk." Garrison scooted all the way back in the large stuffed chair, leaned back and tried to relax. He had not been summoned before by Thurston since he arrived at the Fort three weeks earlier and he was more than a little nervous.

The papers Thurston was shuffling through was Garrison's folder. Since this was his first assignment since graduation from the Point, there was not much to look at. "I see you were third in your class Lieutenant."

"Yes Sir."

Thurston closed the folder. "You've been here what, three weeks now, Lieutenant?" Thurston asked.

"Almost Sir. Been here two weeks and three days."

Thurston knew exactly how long he had been here. He was just getting him to talk, to relax some. A good Post Commander would know everything about his officers. Things such as their strengths, weaknesses, and even their private life. He knew Garrison had a top rating from the Point but that didn't mean squat out here. He also knew how it was for a young officer to sit down and talk to his Commanding Officer, especially if that Commanding Officer thought he was a little above everyone else. Thurston had one like that once when he was young and he swore he would never be like that if he ever received a command. He would always be approachable, from the officers to the enlisted men. He knew the only way he would ever get good answers, and not necessarily the ones he wanted to hear, was to have whomever he was talking to relaxed, not afraid to speak. Even the lowest private in this mans army may have a idea that would benefit all out in this desolate territory.

"You have not led a patrol as of yet have you, Lieutenant?"

"No Sir. I was an observer last week with Lt. Mandrel on a two- day patrol."

"Before we discuss your patrol in the morning, Lieutenant, I want you to understand one thing.."

"Yes Sir." Garrison said leaning forward in the chair.

"I'm going to give you some advice that, if you take to heart, just may help you to make it out here. A lot of you young officers come out here with a chip on your shoulder. They think they know it all and won't listen to some of the old veterans that's been around for awhile. They go strictly by the book, no variance at all. I know what is taught at the Point but understand this, Lieutenant. What you learned at the Point, no matter how correct you may think it is, is for the most part not worth a tinker's damn out here. The bandits have never read a book on how to fight a war. They make their own rules and they are vicious. The Apaches, now they are something else again. While you were playing with your toys as a kid, an Apache child was learning to track, shoot, and hunt. By the time they are in their early teens, they are usually battle tested, counted coup and killed an enemy. They can't read a word of English but they can track a lizard over rocks. They can come into your camp after you have left, tell how many of you there were, how many horses you had, when you arrived and when you left, and probably what you ate. They have been surviving in this harsh land for a hundred years and they have become part of it. What I'm trying to emphasize, Mr. Garrison, is do not underestimate the Apache just because he has no education."

"Yes Sir. I understand, Sir."

"Another thing Lieutenant." Thurston continued. "Learn the lay of the land, where the springs are and where the easy trails are. This land can kill you as quick and as sure as a bandit's bullet or an Apache's arrow. Going with you in the morning is First Sergeant O'Malley. He has picked the men for the patrol. He is a good man and knows his business. Listen to him. Ask questions. When you have a chance, visit with the scout, Watkins. He is the best there is and he can help you a lot." Thurston stood up and walked over to the map on the wall. "Come over to the map, Lieutenant." As Garrison come up behind him, Thurston pointed to a spot on the map. "Do you know what this is?"

Garrison looked at where Thurston's finger was. "Yes Sir, that's the Old San Antonio/San Diego Mail Road."

"Somewhere on that road, between here," placing his finger on Fort Clark," and there," placing a finger on Fort Inge, "is a overdue pay wagon and Tye Watkins. Your orders is to find the pay wagon and Watkins and get them here as quickly as possible. You will leave before daylight in the morning. Are there any questions?"

"No Sir. "

"Then find Sergeant O'Malley and get the final details straightened out."

"Yes Sir, Major." Garrison saluted and turned to leave but was stopped by Thurston's voice.

"One more thing, Lieutenant. Remember what I said about listening and watching. Don't be afraid to ask questions. Your rank will get your orders followed but to get the men to go that extra step, to have faith in your decisions, will have to come in time. Make good sound decisions and don't get men killed unnecessarily and you will earn their respect. That is what you will have to earn, their respect."

"Yes sir, I will do as you suggested. This, being out here, is all I have ever wanted." He turned and left.

"We'll see." Thurston said. "We'll see." He turned and walked to his office window and looked out across the parade ground.

~

Garrison headed for O'Malley's quarters more excited, or maybe it was nervous, than he had ever been in his life. This was his chance to prove to everyone, himself included, that he belonged out here. Three months ago he would never had dreamed he would be in this position. With his father's connections in Washington, he was sure he would end up assigned somewhere back East. He hadn't figured out how he got himself assigned to this God forsaken country.

His father was a successful business man and being the only child, he had never been without anything he wanted. Being a rich kid he was picked on by some of the other boys and had to learn to defend himself at a early age. He entered the army to try and get away from his doting parents for awhile, to prove to himself he make it own his own. He never dreamed he would be this far away though.

~

Frank, Miguel, and Jesus had all the men back at their camp rolling with laughter, telling of the stupid gringo who was shaking their hands and thanking them for saving his life as they bashed his head in... all except Alex that is. He suspected there was more to this gringo than they knew. From the way Frank said the man handled himself with the Apaches, he wasn't just another gringo who happened to pass that way.

"Hey Frank, what did this, as you call him, stupid gringo look like and how was he dressed?" he asked.

"Just a gringo Alex, maybe taller'n most," Frank answered and turned back to face the men he was entertaining.

"Dammit, don't make me ask again, Frank," Alex shouted threateningly.

"Okay, Okay, " Frank said. "He was maybe two or three inches over six foot. He wore a buckskin shirt and cavalry pants."

"He wore knee high moccasin boots like the Apache wear," Jesus added. "And his saddle and blanket were army issue."

"Miguel, get me the gun and belt you took." Alex said.

"Why you so interested in this gringo, Alex. Hell, we left him in the middle of nowhere with no weapon. He'll probably die anyway from the bashed in head Jesus gave him," Frank said laughing.

Miguel returned with the gun belt and gun and handed them to Alex who had taken a seat on his blankets. He turned them over in his hands until he found what he expected to find... the initials TW. He slowly stood up and faced Frank. Doubling up his fist, and as quick as a rattlesnakes strike, hit Frank square on the chin that lifted him off the ground and deposited him on his back. Frank's hot Mexican blood was boiling. He reached for his gun only to see Alex holding a gun and pointing it straight at his chest.

"What's wrong with you, are you crazy or what?" Frank shouted and stood up taking his hand away from his gun.

"You made two big mistakes today. One, by not killing this so called stupid gringo when you had the chance. This gringo you call stupid, is the Chief of Scouts at Fort Clark, Tye Watkins. All the men looked at each other and understood why Alex was so upset. They all had heard the stories about Tye, and to the man, didn't want no part of him.

"The second mistake you made was leaving those dead Apaches there. I tried to make it look like the Apaches had done this thing. Everyone knows that Apaches don't just leave without taking their dead with them. I can promise you, Frank, Watkins will survive this if for no other reason, than to hunt you down and kill you."

"How's he going to do this? He doesn't know who I am or where I went," Frank said confidently.

"Can you fly like a bird Frank? If you can't, then you left tracks and Watkins can track a ghost. When he was with the Rangers, he tracked so many bandits down that a bounty was put on him. No one could collect it. He'll find you and when he does, he'll find the rest of us. I can't risk that. You three get on your horses and ride out. I don't care where you go nor do I want to know. Just get the hell out of here… NOW."

"But Alex," Frank started to argue but Alex had turned his back and was walking off. He watched for a minute and then, looking at the others for second, shrugged his shoulders and shook his head. The three of them left, heading northwest, toward Brackettville, and Fort Clark. Shortly thereafter, Alex and the rest rode west toward their hideout on the Rio Grande River. He had hated to do that to his brother, but you didn't take a chance with a man like Watkins. He nor any other bandito wanted that man on their trail. He wasn't kidding when he told Frank that Tye was not dead nor would he die. He knew men like that. Men who, when they had a purpose, would not be stopped. He wasn't afraid of Watkins but he sure as hell wanted no part of him if he could avoid it.

~

Tanza and Lone Wolfe had to stop when it became too dark to follow the youngster's tracks. They made camp not knowing they were less than a mile from where Two Bears and his friends lay. They sat on their blankets and talked of the days not so long ago. Days when they roamed the mountains and the land beyond as they wished. They lived to hunt, and to raid the Comanche and Kiowa camps for horses and slaves. This had been and always would be, as long as they live, the Apaches' way of life. They fell asleep listening to the night sounds of the desert, the owls screeching, the beat of the bats wings as they flew looking for insects, and the woeful sound of a coyotes' howling. They slept soundly knowing their nearby horses would alert them of anyone or anything coming close to their camp.

~

It was close to midnight when Tye stopped to rest. He figured he had covered about seven miles so far and had just about wore his neck out from turning to look over his shoulder… looking for the Apaches he expected to see coming after him.

"Thank you, Lord, for a moonless night," he said. His tracks would be hard to follow this night.

He was sitting on a large boulder, rubbing his feet thru his moccasins. He was thinking that this infantry stuff is a lot of crap. He looked up at the heavens and the countless stars and picked out a couple of constellations his father had showed him. He still thought of his parents a lot. They had been very loving parents--and he missed them. He wished they were here to meet Rebecca. He knew they would have liked her. He stood up, took a good drink of water, and was off again realizing a breeze had come up and it was actually getting chilly.

"Only in this part of the world can you fry your butt during the day and freeze it at night," he said then wondered how in hell a man could still have a sense of humor after what he had been through today.

◆ V ◆

Frank and his companions, riding hard, arrived in Brackettville late that night. Being familiar with the country, they had cut across the land, not using the road which was the longer route. The town was a mixture of wooden and adobe shanty's. There was a general store and two saloons. The population, mostly Mexican with a few trappers thrown in, totaled about two hundred. Of course you had the troops at Fort Clark just across the road which also numbered close to two hundred. The town had been named for a man named Brackett shortly after the Fort was founded in 1852. It was a prosperous little town being the only place the soldiers could spend their pay, plus being the only place within a twenty or so mile radius that the settlers could find supplies.

Coming in off the trail, the three men headed to the nearest saloon. When they entered, the patrons gave them the once over and then went back to what they were doing. The bar extended the entire length of one side of the room. There were six or seven tables on the other side. One of the tables were occupied by two men and a couple of "ladies". There were two men at the bar, leaning with their backs against the bar. Like most saloons there was a large mirror behind the bar and a picture of a nude woman above it. , The place smelled of cigarette smoke, stale sweat, and smelly brass spittoons that were located in various places on the floor. Otherwise, it was clean, with the floor being swept and the glasses stacked neat and clean.

"Howdy boys," the bartender said. He had three whiskeys on a tray and set one in front of each man.

"First drink is on the house for first time customers and since I ain't seen you before, I reckon you qualify,' he added, smiling.

"Gracious" both Jesus and Miguel said at the same time.

Frank didn't say anything as his mind was on a pretty black haired girl that was at the table with two men who appeared, by their dress, to be trappers. She was soliciting drinks and whatever else she could. She looked up and saw the handsome Frank and winked. That was all the incentive he needed and he started over but was abruptly stopped by a strong hand gripping his arm and turning him around.

"What in the hell do you think you are doing grabbing me like that?" he hissed at Miguel.

"Trying to keep my friend out of trouble," Miguel said.

"Trouble, I ain't in no trouble," replied Frank.

"That man the girl is sitting with does not look the type to appreciate someone butting in right now. There would be trouble," Miguel said flatly.

"Then I kill him. How about that? Then there won't be no more trouble," Frank declared.

"Either way you lose, Frank," Miguel calmly stated.

"What you mean, either way I lose?"

"You and him fight, He kills you, you lose. You kill him, you will lose because the authorities will investigate and what you gonna say Frank, when they ask you where you got all that money?"

Frank, looking at his friend for a moment, put his hand on Miguel's shoulder and said,

"You are right amigo, lets just get drunk and have a good time. There will be plenty of time for whores later." They did.

~

Garrison had tossed and turned all night, thinking of nothing but his first patrol. He kept going over things he needed to do again and again, not wanting to forget anything. Walking out of his quarters just before dawn he was shocked to see O'Malley and the patrol, in formation, facing him, ready to go. A stable boy had his horse saddled and waiting for him.

"The patrol is ready to leave, Lieutenant." O'Malley said.

"Very well Sgt.," Garrison said as he mounted and turned his horse, "By the twos then."

"By the twos," O'Malley shouted and the patrol formed two a breast. "Forward, Yo," he said raising and dropping his arm. They started out at a walk, sitting tall in the saddle and shoulders squared, and as they passed Thurston on his porch, Garrison saluted. Thurston returned the salute and held it until the last man had passed.

"Double time Sgt." Garrison stated.

O'Malley pumped his arm twice and the patrol was off at a canter. The Flag, making a snapping sound as it fluttered in the breeze, caused Garrison to turn at the sound and looked up at the Flag. He had never felt taller and prouder.

"The men look sharp Sergeant." he said.

"Hand picked'um my own self," O'Malley said proudly. "All good men. Didn't figure the Lieutenant needed the problems on his first patrol that green troops can cause," he added.

After about fifteen minutes they slowed to a walk. Garrison liked O'Malley right off and could see why Thurston thought so highly of him. He planned on visiting a lot with him on this patrol, picking his brain for information. For now though, he would just study the lay of the land and get a feel for where things were. There was a slight breeze this morning, but you could already see that it was going to be another typical July day, hot and dry. In looking at this land, there wasn't much top soil so the grass was sparse and short. It was called grama grass. It would take a lot of land to feed even a small herd of cattle. The land looked to rocky and hard for farming. ' Why in Gods' name are all these people coming out here to settle,' he wondered.

"Bout two miles yonder," O'Malley said pointing, " is a spring that always has water in it. Nothing like Los Moras Springs at the Fort or Val Verde Springs at Camp Val Verde though," he added. " You need to make a mental map of places like that Lieutenant. Can't ever tell when you may need them if you get in a tight spot."

"When was this road built that we're on?" Garrison asked.

"Lets see," O'Malley said pausing to spit a wad of tobacco juice at a lizard sitting on a rock, "I think it was built back in the early fifties. It runs from San Antonio thru Inge, Clark, Camp Verde then swings north up to Ft. Davis. From there , El Paso and on west to San Diego. It's kept up pretty well because of the stage line using it. Man or mail, can make the trip from San Antonio to San Diego in thirty days or so if there ain't no problems." They rode for a few more minutes in silence before Garrison spoke.

"Tell me about Tye Watkins. I understand you know him pretty well."

"Yes sir, I know him as well as anyone, better'n most I guess. He's courting my niece you know."

"So I've heard. I have heard some stories that are hard to believe about him. Maybe you can sort out what's true and what's not."

"Well," O'Malley said rubbing his chin thinking. "First off, the stories you heard are probably true. There's plenty of them to tell. Tye was born about 1839 and raised about twenty-five miles southwest of here. His dad, Ben, was a tough hombre. He was a old mountain man and a quite famous one I might add. He started teaching Tye tracking, hunting, and how to survive at a early age. Tye was bigger than most youngsters his age and by the time he was fifteen, he could handle just about any grown man---except Ben. He was an expert tracker by then. He could handle a knife as well as any Apache could. Hell, he could live as well off the land as they could."

"I heard he was commanding a troop of Rangers at the age of twenty or so. Is that true?"

"Yes, at twenty," O'Malley answered.

"That's one of them that's hard to believe, Sgt. . All his men must have been older than him."

"Yes sir, a lot older. The Rangers recruited a lot of men to help protect the countryside from the Apaches and the bandits during the War. All the federal troops were pulled out and sent back East to fight. The frontier was left unprotected so the Rangers were formed. Some called them the Texas Mounted Rifles. Ben and Tye joined up. The Rangers were a tough lot, being mostly trappers, ex- buffalo hunters, and the like. Ben was killed in a battle shortly there-after. Part of his mother died the day they buried Ben. She was just never the same after that. She died less than a year later of a fever. Seems this all changed Tye and he put all his efforts in catching bandits and killing Apaches not really caring if he lived or died. The older men had learned to respect his fighting and tracking skill. His disregard for his own hide in order to save some men during an ambush on the Devils River in about "63 started the stories about him. He displayed a good head on his shoulders and was fearless. This got the attention of his superiors, and he was promoted. I'll tell you something else, those old men would go to hell and get ole Lucifer his self if he asked them to. That's how much they respected him. Hell, he tracked down so many damn bandits, that the bandits put a bounty on him at one time."

'Amazing how often that word, 'respect', comes up out here,' Garrison thought.

◆ VI ◆

Tye had walked until the sun was well over the top of the hills. He spotted a group of extremely large boulders about two hundred yards north of the road. Walking to them he found a shady spot, and after checking for critters, lay down in the shade. One of the critters he was looking for was rattlesnakes. On hot days they like the shade also and he wasn't to fond of the idea of curling up with one of them. He would stay here till late afternoon and then start his walk toward Clark again. He was asleep in a few minutes.

~

Tanza was holding the body of Two Bears in his arms. He looked at the bodies of the other two boys, then what was left of the troopers. He had seen a lot during his years of warring, but nothing compared to this. This was almost too much for even him to handle. He walked to the wagon and gently placed Two Bears in the shade, under the wagon. Keeling beside his brother, he placed his hand on Two Bears chest.

"The ones who did this will pay with their lives, my brother. But before they die, they will die a thousand deaths, this I swear to you."

Lone Wolf brought the bodies of White Owl and Two Moons and placed them beside their friend. He and Tanza then walked in different directions looking for signs. After a few minutes they had a pretty good picture of what happened, but one thing they could not figure out was, why one man was walking, and the others riding off in a different direction. They also found the track with a notched shoe.

"Lone Wolf, ride back to the camp and bring the others here." Tanza said. "Have someone take care of our brothers," nodding his head toward the dead, "And then follow me. I am going to see where the three men are going. I will wait on the trail for you to join me." .

As Lone Wolf rode away, Tanza mounted his pony and started following the tracks. He already had a hate in his gut for the white man and now it was reaching the boiling point and was due to boil over any second. It would not be pretty if he accidentally bumped into a white or Mexican man right now.

~

Garrison's patrol was moving again after taking a short break. It was past midmorning and the heat was mounting. The tunics the men wore had to have been made by a man who loved to see men suffer. They were of heavy wool, not necessarily the best material for one hundred degree plus days. Garrison still could not believe how anyone or anything would want to live in this country. It was good for the mesquite and the cactus and that was about all. He was amazed though, at the amount of wildlife that was in this arid land. He had already seen several deer and one bunch of antelope. Rabbits were abundant and he saw two strange looking critters that looked pretty fearsome. O'Malley said they were wild hogs and could be dangerous when wounded. O'Malley was naming off different animals that existed here, coyotes, wolves, badgers, and an occasional bear and panthers, were among many others he named .Garrison shook his head disbelieving that so much wildlife could survive in this country.

This land will sort of grow on you, Lieutenant." O'Malley said. "I know how you feel right now because me and every man in this patrol felt the same way at first. This land never changes. It's the same now as it was a hundred years ago and will be the same a hundred years from now. You'll wake up one day and realize this land has a beauty of its own. Not a majestic beauty like the high mountains, but a rugged beauty

Garrison laughed. "I don't know, Sergeant. It's not very appealing right now."

O'Malley, with the ever present chew in his mouth spit and laughed. "It will, Lieutenant, it will." Then he thought to himself. 'If you live long enough.'

~

Tye woke up suddenly and it took a minute for him to figure out why. He was hot...hot and sweating. He was now lying in the sun as his shade had left him and it was hot and the sun reflecting off the rocks only added to the heat. He stood up to find some more shade and glanced toward the road. He was surprised to see a dust cloud on the road. He slid back into the shade of the boulders and waited to see who it was. He was praying it wasn't the Apaches. No way would they miss seeing his tracks leaving the road heading toward these boulders. It was a long five minutes before he saw the Flag waving above the dust, then the blue tunics of cavalry. He took out his Bowie and using the blade as a mirror, flashed the patrol.

"What do you make of it, O'Malley." Garrison asked.

"Dunno Lieutenant, but someone is trying hard to get our attention," O'Malley answered. "Do you want me to take a man and see what or who it is?"

"Huh, yes, Sergeant, be careful," Garrison stuttered.

O'Malley and the trooper rode at a gallop toward the boulders. He stopped short of them to take a better look before barging in. He almost had a heart attack when he heard his name called.

"O'Malley, you old cuss, I'm damn glad to see you," a voice was saying from somewhere in the boulders. Suddenly a man appeared.

"My God, is that you Tye? " O'Malley said not believing his eyes.

"Yep, its me, what's left anyway. You had me worried there for a minute, O'Malley."

"How's that," O'Malley asked dismounting and hurrying to meet him.

"The way you was coming I didn't figure you was going to stop and look around. Thought you'd forgot everything I taught you," Tye said smiling. "What in the world is going on anyway?" O'Malley asked, looking at Tye's condition.

"Tell you in a minute," Tye said. "Got anything to eat. My ole' belly ain't seen nothing but water since yesterday before I left the Fort."

O'Malley, digging in his saddlebags. "Got nothing but hardtack and biscuit."

"When you're as hungry as I am Sarge, that sounds like steak and potatoes."

O'Malley had sent the trooper back to get Garrison. When they arrived, the Lieutenant made a beeline for Tye.

"Mr. Watkins , I need a report on what is going on," he ordered.

Tye, with a mouthful of dry biscuit was silent, sitting on a boulder and looking at the ground.

"I need to know what is going on, NOW, Mr. Watkins," he said again.

O'Malley stepped between them, "Would the Lieutenant step over there with me for a moment, sir?" he asked nodding toward the horses.

Lieutenant Garrison, his dandruff up, looked away from the top of Tye's head and at O'Malley and back at Tye. "Very Well, Sergeant." He said not taking his eyes off Tye.

Off to the side and out of earshot O'Malley said, "Lieutenant, if you'll be a little patient and let the man eat, you will get your report. He hasn't eaten anything in over twenty- four hours and if you look at him, must have been thru some kind of hell."

Garrison turned and looked just as Tye raised his head. He saw for the first time what O'Malley was talking about.

He walked over to Tye offering his hand, "I hope you will overlook my over exuberance a few minutes ago. I was not aware of what you have been through."

Tye smiled, shook his hand and told him," Sit down, Lieutenant, and as soon as my stomach quits growling I'll fill you in on everything." He finished in a couple of minutes and gave the Lieutenant a complete run down of what had happened.

"Why do you suppose there were only an escort of four men?" he asked looking at Tye.

"Same question I asked the Major, Lieutenant, but not as nicely as you just did," he replied with a slight grin. "O'Malley, you got an extra mount and maybe a gun I can use?"

"I sure as hell can find you one," O'Malley replied.

"What do you need a weapon for Mr. Watkins? Aren't you going to the Fort hospital for medical help?" Garrison asked.

"Nope, going to find that payroll and the men that left me for dead "Tye said, walking off.

Garrison stood there looking at him walking off and not believing what he just heard.

"Told you he was as tough as nails Lieutenant. I wouldn't want to be one of those men when he catches up with them either." O'Malley said. "He can be meaner than an Apache when his dandruff is up."

"I see what you mean Sgt," Garrison said and shook his head.

Tye was given a horse and a rifle and a sidearm with belt and holster.

"Strange how it makes you feel different when armed," he thought to himself. "I never realized how naked I felt without them till now." Feeling much better after filling his stomach, he mounted up and was ready when the rest of the patrol was.

"I sent a rider back with a dispatch to Thurston, filling him in on what you told me and that we were in pursuit of the Apaches responsible, Garrison said.

"Thurston needed to know about what happened," Tye replied, "but I don't think the Apaches were responsible."

"I thought you said the troopers were scalped and had arrows in them." he said, while looking questionably at Tye and then at O'Malley.

"They were scalped and shot with arrows, Lieutenant, just like I said. But I didn't have time to really look around before the Apaches shot my horse," Tye said. "There were a lot of shod ponies there and boot tracks. I have learned never to take anything for granted. Never believe all that you hear and read. Only believe what you see and know is a fact."

"Why would someone, a white man, do an unbelievable thing like that to another white man? Garrison asked, shaking his head in disbelief.

"Wouldn't be the first time that the blame was put on the Apaches for something they didn't do." Tye said, while looking at the road ahead. "I didn't say it was a white man either. Could have been Mexican bandits. There are more Mexican bandit gangs around here than white."

They rode in silence for a few minutes before Tye left, taking his customary position about a quarter of mile in front. He thought he had seen something in the distance when he was talking with the Lieutenant a few minutes ago. When he arrived to about where he figured it was, he saw some antelope moving off in the distance and figured it was them he saw crossing the road. Looking back at the patrol, he could see the first two or three men and the rest were in a cloud of dust from the road. There was no breeze to blow the stuff away. He knew the men toward the back were miserable in the choking stuff. He looked to the west and, for the first time in days, actually saw some clouds that may be moving in.

"Lord, if those are rain clouds, hold them off till I get a chance to see what happened and get a fix on where the men that butchered those troopers are headed before you wipe out the tracks, okay." he asked prayerfully. Then he thought. 'I've talked to the Lord more in the last two days than in my whole life. No reason for Him to help someone out that only talks to Him when they want something either.' A slight breeze began blowing from the southwest and helped keep the dust down and off the men and horses.

"You say all the stories are true that I have heard about him?" Garrison asked nodding toward Tye.

"Yes sir." O'Malley replied. "I have seen too many things he has done not to believe all of them."

"Is it true about his father being a pretty well know mountain man?"

"Back in the late twenties and early thirties, he teamed up with Jim Bridger, and Shakespeare McDovitt. They had lot of stories written about them, mostly about Bridger though. Ben, that's Tye's pa, said it was because Bridger could tell tales better than they could." O'Malley answered chuckling.

BORDER TROUBLE 49

About mid afternoon Tye saw the buzzards. He waited until the patrol caught up. "Lieutenant, this is not going to be a pretty sight and I want to scout the area a little more before more tracks are added. Can you take your men and go there," he said, pointing to a spot south of the road. They will be up wind there and the horses will not be so skittish. He dismounted and handed his reins to O'Malley and started walking toward the mound of buzzards.

As he got close, the buzzards started flapping their wings and generally getting upset that this intruder was back. All finally flew away leaving something that Tye had never hoped to see again. The bodies, if you could call them that, were in bits and pieces. He heard a noise behind and turned to see Garrison losing what little he had on his stomach. Embarrassed, Garrison apologized, "Sorry about that, Tye. It was a lot worse than I expected--and the smell, my God."

"Don't be embarrassed, Lieutenant. I promise you, before this day is complete, just about every man will lose it. Take your bandana and go over to the water barrel and wet it and wrap it around your mouth and nose. It'll help some." Give me ten minutes to look around and then bring your men in,"

Tye noticed right off that a lot of unshod ponies had been here since he left and the dead youngsters were gone. He made a wide circle and found the track he was looking for, the one with the notch. He also saw a lot of unshod ponies were following them. He made his way back to where the men were cleaning up the carnage.

"I had the remains put into the wagon and O'Malley has assigned two men to hitch their horses to it and take them back to the Fort along with my report of what has happened up to now," Garrison told Tye.

"Good. Lieutenant. Why don't you cover them with some dirt." Tye suggested. "That will help some with the stench and the horses will be easier to control.. They will have enough trouble with them anyway with their not ever being in a harness before," The wagon headed back and the patrol was following Tye, who was having no trouble following the tracks of twenty or so horses.

~

Tanza followed the tracks right into the canyon and was surprised he didn't know it was there. He thought he knew all the water holes in this part of the country. Going back outside of the hidden entrance he found two sets of tracks, three headed northwest and eight or nine headed west. The tracks he wanted, the one with the notch, were headed northwest. He followed the tracks for over a hour until he was sure where they were headed to. He went back to the draw to wait for Lone Wolf and did not have to wait long. The braves were angry, wanting blood for their lost brothers. They formed a circle around Tanza and waited for him to speak. Tanza looked at each brave before speaking.

"I have been following the tracks of the men who done this deed to our brothers." He pointed to the ground. "See the track with the cut in it. Do not forget it. One of the men who killed them rides this horse. The men we are after are headed for the village called Brackett. Only one trail goes into the village and one trail out. When they leave, we will have them. We will stay hidden and watch all people traveling the trail and after they pass, we will check their tracks for the one we look for. I want two of you on both trails. When you find them, one will follow and the other will come and get the rest of us. Control yourselves. Do not kill anyone or let your presence be known."

Tanza was pleased that his friend, Lone Wolf, was the first to say he would take the trail from the village west toward Val Verde Springs. Others volunteered quickly. The four left to make their way the several miles to take their positions on the road. Tanza and the rest headed toward their camp on the Rio Grande.

~

It was dusk when the patrol found the vacated camp in the hidden draw. Tye had scouted the area outside of the draw and found where the three had headed for Brackettville and where the larger group headed west, probably going to Mexico. He also saw the Apache tracks, four or five following the three men and the others going west. Tye went back into the draw where they were going to camp for the night. The strong aroma of hot coffee was in the air along with the smell of bacon frying. He had not realized how hungry he was until now.

After eating biscuits and bacon, O'Malley, Garrison, and Tye were sitting on their bedrolls talking, drinking coffee.

"When do you think we will catch up with the Apaches?" Garrison asked.

O'Malley and Tye looked at each other and, when Tye rolled his eyes, O'Malley had to turn his head to keep Garrison from seeing him laugh.

"Do you still think the Apaches ambushed the pay wagon, Lieutenant?" Tye asked.

"Well..yes," he answered . "We have been following their tracks all afternoon, haven't we?"

"Yes, but only because they were following the tracks we were following," Tye answered.

"What tracks? I don't know what you are talking about. I thought we were after the Apaches. They were there."

"Yes, they were. However, the Apaches were there after the ambush. As a matter of fact, they were not there until this morning. Mexicans took the payroll, Lieutenant, and they have a several hour head start on us and are headed to Mexico. The ambush was made to look like the Apaches did it," Tye explained.

"Are you absolutely sure Tye?" he asked.

"Look at it this way, Lieutenant. The Apaches have no need for money. Where are they going to spend it? That scalping job was the worst I ever saw. A blind Apache would have done a better job. When I arrived there yesterday, shod tracks were everywhere. Today, you saw some unshod tracks made by Apaches, but they came looking for the youngsters, and were made earlier today. The good news is that three of the men I think were in on the ambush are apparently headed for Brackettville and the Fort. I think at daybreak we should head back to the Fort and maybe find them there but that's just a suggestion, Sir..

They lay on their bedrolls, each with his own thoughts, listening to the night sounds of the desert, the footfalls of the sentinels as they marched back and forth, and the noise made by the horses as they munched their oats and the short grama grass. Each finally drifted off to sleep.

Border Trouble

~

The patrol arrived back at the Fort about four in the afternoon. O'Malley took Tye's and Garrison's horses, so they could report immediately to Thurston. Tye reported first, then asked if there was anything else. There wasn't, so he excused himself and told them he was headed to town and see if anyone had seen his three, ' friends'. Thurston demanded he see the Fort surgeon first and get his head doctored. At the surgeon's office Tye's head wound was taken care of and when he removed his shirt so the bullet burn on his shoulder could be looked at the surgeon was amazed at the number of scars.

"You'll never die, Tye. From the look of all these wounds you must not have any vital organs." he said shaking his head. When Tye came back by Thurston's office, Thurston wanted to send a couple of men with him into Brackettville but Tye talked him out of it.

He got no information out of the bartender and patrons in the first saloon. Jim, the bartender and owner of the second saloon was a friend of his and Tye knew he would tell him if he knew anything. He was right, The three had been in last night but he hadn't seen them today. Tye thanked him and headed to the stables where he found the horse with the notched shoe. They were here alright and Tye could feel the fire starting to burn inside him. It would have to wait though, he had a dance to go to.

~

After bathing, shaving, and putting on some clean clothes he headed for O'Malley's. He was still thirty yards away when Rebecca came running out to meet him and throwing her arms around his neck.

"Tye, oh Tye, I was so worried after those poor troopers were brought in yesterday." She tried holding back the tears but they came anyway. He kissed her and tasted the slightly salty taste of her tears on her lips. He pulled back touching his lips with his finger.

"Sun burned lips doesn't feel none to good kissing." He said laughing.

"Well then." She said. "We just won't kiss." He reached around her with his arms and pulled her tightly against him. "I'll just have to suffer." And he kissed her again. They parted from each other slightly and she gingerly felt of the knot on the side of his head and looked him over, head to foot.

Watching her he asked," Does everything look okay?"

"Huh, oh yes" she said embarrassed, then she laughed.

"I know you told me not to worry and I didn't, until those men arrived yesterday in the wagon." She placed her head against his chest. "I never dreamed anything could be so horrible."

"I know, I was hoping you would not see it." Let's change the subject," he said. "What time do I pick you up to go to the dance?"

"Well, the games start in about a hour, but if it's okay with you, lets just eat and go to the dance." she said.

"Fine, I'll see you about seven then," he said and kissed her on the cheek and left.

◆ VII ◆

A social event out here was a big event. There weren't many opportunities for people to get together due to distances and other factors. An event like this one will draw people from twenty, thirty miles away. It was a chance for the young people to mingle with others their age and compete in various games. It was a opportunity for the men to hoist a beer or two, renew old friendships, and discuss all the current events. The women would sit and visit and, of course, catch up on the latest gossip. Tye figured the main reason everyone came was that for a day or two they could relax and not be looking for trouble over their shoulder. It was a chance to let the strain of constant vigilance and everyday hardships that these people lived with go away for awhile.

Everyone would attend the dance after the evening cookout. A dance would be one of the few times you would see a man in this country without a sidearm. They were collected and held till the man left. There were always fights at these socials. Anytime you mix beer and men there were always differences of opinions. At least with no firearms, damage would be held to a minimum.

The meal was great... plenty of beef, bacon, and some pork. There was corn on the cob, beans, onions, and potatoes. Even the Fort bakery got in on the act by baking some delicious pastries. The dance started about eight thirty. Tye and Rebecca had danced every dance so far and now, they both wanted some refreshments and to catch their breath. They returned to their table only to find Garrison and Thurston sitting there, both standing up when Rebecca started to sit.

"Tye, you look a heck of a lot different than earlier today," Garrison said, laughing.

"It's amazing what a razor and a little soap and water will do for a man, ain't it," Tye answered smiling and shaking both men's hands.

Tye introduced Rebecca to Lieutenant Garrison who gave her an elaborate bow, surprising Rebecca.

"You are more beautiful up close than you are from a distance." He said.

"Thank you, Lieutenant." Rebecca said. "That's quite nice of you."

"Looks like just about every homesteader in the area is here." Thurston said.

"I didn't know this many people lived out here." Garrison stated looking around.

Suddenly, there was a commotion across the dance floor and people were rushing to see what was going on.

"I wondered how long it would take for a fight to start," Thurston stated.

The four of them went to where the commotion was and saw two Mexicans beating the hell out of a white man who must have been in his late fifties or early sixties.

"Sonofabitch," Tye hollered racing in and grabbing one of the Mexicans. He swung him around to face him and came with a right that caught the surprised man on the chin and lifted him in the air for several feet and deposited him at the feet of some of the spectators.

"YOU,." the other Mexican shouted as he turned to see who had hit his friend. "You are supposed to be dead."

"Not hardly, you bastard" and Tye hit him a glancing blow that opened a cut on the man's cheek.

A gasp came from the onlookers when the Mexican pulled a Bowie out of his belt and swiped at Tye's belly. Almost caught flat footed, Tye stepped back and sucked his belly in. The blade missed by a half a inch. He reached for his Bowie that was in his boot and they both circled each other in a crouch, knives in their right hands. Two troopers started in to help but Tye waved them back. Tye feinted a swipe and the Mexican flinched but didn't step back. Tye knew from many a knife fight that this man wasn't much at handling a knife. He knew what was coming and he was ready. After one more complete circle the Mexican took a vicious swipe again and Tye deftly stepped back and brought his knife down, slicing deep into the Mexican's forearm causing him to drop the knife. The Mexican screamed in pain, pressed his left hand on top of the cut trying to stop the blood when Tye hit him flush on the nose, breaking it and splattering blood everywhere. The fight was gone from the Mexican but not from Tye. He grabbed his shirt collar and jerked him and planted a right fist on the man's chin. Tye let the now unconscious man fall to the ground. The two troopers picked him up and a third trooper took the other Mexican who was now semi-awake, to the guardhouse. The army surgeon was dispatched to look after his wound.

Tye walked over to the elderly man and made sure he was okay. A girl, about fourteen or fifteen, probably his daughter, thanked Tye and kissed him on the cheek, embarrassing Tye. The old man, the young girl, and Tye talked for a minute before Tye walked back to where Rebecca, Garrison, and the Major were.

"What was that all about?" Thurston asked.

"That was two of the sonofab"...then remembering Rebecca, "two of the men that left me for dead. One of them was the one that bashed me on the head. They were pestering the young girl and when the old man tried to stop them, they jumped him.

"You think they were in on the ambush?" Thurston asked.

"I'd bet my life on it, Major. It was just too coincidental that they showed up when they did yesterday. They are obviously scum for what they did to me and to that old man tonight. Yeah, I'm sure."

"Well, we have them and can question them later. They aren't going anywhere so let's forget them for a while and have a good time," Thurston said.

The band was playing again and the fight, as usual, was quickly forgotten as couples moved to the dance floor. Tye and Rebecca sat this one out and were enjoying their refreshments, Tye, his beer, and Rebecca, her lemonade.

"Sorry you had to see that, honey. I sorta lost it when I saw those two, "He said.

She put her hand on top of his and gave him that 'everything is okay' look. Actually, she got excited watching him in action. She had only heard stories before about Tye's ability to handle any situation, now she knew they were true.

"I wonder where the third one was?" Garrison asked.

"I bet we can find out, can't we, Tye," Thurston said winking at Tye. "After you have taken Rebecca home, stop by my quarters to discuss this further. Now, if you will excuse me, I have to make the rounds and then I'm going to my quarters. Goodnight, Miss O'Malley. It's always a pleasure to be around you. Goodnight, Mr. Garrison and I'll see you later, Tye."

"What do you think he meant by that remark, Tye?" Rebecca asked.

"What remark?"

"That you and him will get the man to talk."

"I guess we'll sit down and visit with him and politely ask him questions as nice as we can. After all, we're civilized. Do you think me, of all people, would be anything but nice," Tye said looking throwing his hands up and looking very innocent.

She looked at him for a moment and saw he was putting her on. "I don't think I want to know anymore about it."

Tye, standing up, asked, "Are you rested enough to dance?' and extended his hand which she took.

They danced and danced and had a great time. Later, on the porch, they were holding each other as tight as possible.

"I was scared at first tonight when that awful man pulled his knife, but then I heard Major Thurston tell Garrison that the Mexican just made a big mistake. He did, didn't he." Tye kissed her hard and long. He could feel every inch of her body pressed against him and he wanted her like never before. She could feel him against her and she was weakening, wanting him. As much as Tye wanted her now, a part of him was telling him to wait, that this was the woman he had waited for. Don't make anything cheap out of it.

"Honey, I've been thinking about us a lot lately."

Rebecca was holding her breath in anticipation of what was coming.

"You know I have my place down on the Devils, and I was thin...".

He was interrupted by the door opening and Sergeant O'Malley stepped out and was tremendously embarrassed, not knowing they were there. Backing up and turning to go back inside, he offered his apologies again over his shoulder.

Tye and Rebecca were both laughing at the look on his face when he saw them. She went back into his arms and said," You were saying before we were interrupted."

"That I need to go. It's late and Thurston's waiting," he lied.

"That's not what you were saying," she said, "You were talking about your place on the Devils and about us."

"We'll discuss it tomorrow, I promise. But right now I need to go see the Major."

He took her in his arms again and held her for a moment, then kissed both cheeks, and then full on the mouth.

She watched him leave and knew that it was now just a matter of time before he asked. She was sure of it. She couldn't wait to tell Mrs. O'Malley all about everything that happened tonight. Tye walked to Thurston's quarters thankful in a way that O'Malley had stepped out when he did because he was at a weak moment and was fixing to ask her to marry him. He knew, or at least he thought he knew, that she was the woman he wanted to spend the rest of his life with. He'd fought bandits, brought in the most vicious Apaches around but here he was, scared to death... of a woman. He smiled.

~

Thurston was waiting for Tye when he arrived at his quarters. He had already questioned the Mexicans, and got no information.

"I spoke with them and got nowhere," he said. "You know the rules and regulations that restrict me from doing what I really would like to do. I know they were in on it, both had almost seven hundred dollars on them."

"I figured as much," Tye said.

"Sometimes a commanding officer can't control things he isn't aware of, Mr. Watkins. Would you like to speak with them to see if you can get any information? You'd be alone with them. Like I said, what I don't know can't hurt now can it?" Thurston said and smiled..

"No sir. You sure can't control everything some of us heathens do," Tye said, laughing.

They walked to the guardhouse, seeing no one because of the late hour.

"Halt, who goes there?" came a nervous voice from in front of the guard house.

"Major Thurston and Tye Watkins to see the prisoners," Thurston said.

There was a moment before the voice said," Come forward and be recognized."

They approached and when the guard recognized them he lowered his weapon.

"Sorry, Major," the guard said.

"Sorry, my butt. That was exactly what you were supposed to do Private," Thurston replied sharply. " What's your name son.?"

"Jackson, Sir, Private Sam Houston Jackson," he answered.

"I'll remember," Thurston said. "Your parents name you after General Houston?" he asked.

"Yes Sir. My pa served with him and was at the Battle of San Jacinto when General Sam took down old Santa Anna."

Thurston wondered how many babies in the last thirty or so years had been named after the famous general.

"Mr. Watkins would like to speak to the prisoners Private Jackson-- alone," the Major said.

"Isn't that against regulations sir?" Jackson asked.

"Let's me and you stroll over there and have a smoke," Thurston said, nodding his head toward a low rock wall a few feet away, "And you can tell be about your pa and General Sam."

"What about my post here?" the private asked.

"We can watch from right here." Thurston said as he sat down on the wall.

Tye entered the guard house and found the cells where the prisoners were located. They had been placed in separate cells, and no others were about. The one he had the knife fight with backed against a far wall when Tye entered his cell, shutting the door behind him.

"What you want, gringo?" he asked in a shaking, nervous voice.

Tye walked to the bunk beds and sat on the lower one and was partially invisible because the only light came from a kerosene lamp on the wall outside the cell. Tye pulled the table over directly in front of him like he was going to play a card game. The man was trying hard to see Tye clearly, but could not.

"Bring that chair over here and sit." he ordered the Mexican.

When the man did not move Tye said in a soft voice. "My friend, have you ever seen a man get hit on a nose that has already been broken. They say its almost more pain than a man can bear."

The Mexican picked up the chair and carried it to the table and sat down with his hands flat on the table. The other one was watching thru the bars from the other cell.

"We can make this easy or hard, it's up to you," Tye said. "What is your name?"

The Mexican turned his head and spit on the floor and said nothing.

"So that's how it's going to be, huh." Tye said and as fast as a rattlesnakes strike, his Bowie flashed down and thru the top on the Mexicans hand pinning it to the table. A blood curdling scream came from Miguel's throat. The other Mexican fell across the cell, eyes wide with fear, and sat in a corner trembling, afraid he would be the next one questioned by this crazy gringo.

Private Jackson jumped up at the sound of the scream. "What the hell?'

"It's nothing to worry about, Private. Here, have one of my cigars and tell me more about your pa and General Sam." Thurston said.

Jackson sat back down and started talking but kept looking over toward the guardhouse, wondering what was going on.

Beads of sweat were dripping from the man's forehead as he looked at the top of his hand with the blade thru it. Tye, with his hand on the bowie's handle, asked, "One more time, what is your name?"

Miguel, looking thru eyes filled with pain, "Miguel... Miguel Espinosa," he whispered. "Who is your friend there?" Tye asked, nodding toward the other cell.

"Jesus Valdez," he uttered in a low voice thru gritted teeth. "And the third one, what is his name, and where is he?" he asked.

Miguel hesitated and Tye twisted the knife slightly causing a new rush of pain coursing through Miguel's body.

"Vasquez, Frank Vasquez." he whispered, his face twisted in agony.

"Alex Vasquez's brother," Tye asked.

Miguel only nodded his head up and down.

"Where's he at now? "he asked.

Miguel could no longer talk, as he passed out from the pain. Tye jerked the knife out, wiping the blade on Miguel's shirt, got up and walked out of the cell and into the next one where Jesus cowered in the corner.

"With the black haired whore from the saloon," Jesus said without Tye having to ask anything.

"Where?" Tye asked, not so much a question as a demand.

"At her place, I guess, Frank left with her before we came to the celebration saying he would see us in the morning," Jesus said.

"Did you two have anything to do with the pay wagon ambush? he asked.

There was no immediate answer from Jesus so Tye took a couple strides toward him and pulling his knife out of the sheath.

"Yes, Yes," Jesus hollered. " We were with Frank and Alex when the pay wagon was robbed. But we didn't kill nobody."

"Maybe you had better tell me about it or I might just start remembering what you did to me," pointing to the lump on the side of his head," and start taking it out on you," Tye said in a low, threatening tone..

Jesus looked over at Alex's unconscious frame and at the Bowie in this crazy white man's hands. He started talking.

"We were told there would be no need for any killing but found out that was a lie. Alex and Frank never intended for there to be any one left alive to blame them. We ambushed the escort, catching them by surprise. The driver, probably an old buffalo hunter, made a try for his rifle and Frank shot him from behind. The soldiers were lined up and disarmed and then one by one, shot by Alex. Frank put some arrows in the bodies of one or two of them. They then scalped them. God forgive me for not doing something to stop it."

"God may forgive you, but I won't, you low life, cowardly bastard," and Tye struck him, knocking him down." I promise you only one thing, my friend, that's a quick death at the end of a rope. The good part of it is, at least for me, is that you know it's coming and will have to wait and worry until you walk those steps."

Tye shut the cell doors, locked them and walked outside to face a nervous guard and a curious Major Thurston.

"Got it, Major. One of them had an accident though. You might consider sending old sawbones over to see him in the morning," Tye said. They left with the private still wondering what the hell went on.

"What did you find out?" Thurston asked as soon as they were out of hearing of the private.

"They are members of the Vasquez bunch. The third one that's still here is Frank himself. They told me about the ambush of the pay wagon. Alex had the soldiers lined up, and he shot each one of them one at a time."

Thurston stopped and looked back at the guardhouse. Tye could sense the anger and disgust that was inside of him.

"God in heaven, what kind of man is this?" Thurston said, shaking his head in disbelief.

"No man Major, just an animal that will be dealt with like any rabid animal."

Nothing else was said until they got to Thurston's quarters. Thurston was on the porch looking down at Tye.

"I've had a man placed inside the stable to watch the horses so I would know when they left. You need to get a couple of men and go fin..." He never finished as the sound of gunshots and women screaming was heard from across the creek, in town.

They were both running as hard as they could across the bridge over Los Moras Creek and into Brackettville. Men were milling around one of the saloons and a woman was screaming hysterically on the walkway outside the saloon.

"What happened?" an out of breath Tye asked the first man he came to.

"Dunno," he said, "Something about a Mexican killing one of the whores."

"Where's he at now,": Tye demanded.

"Someone said he headed for the stables," he answered.

Tye and Thurston made a beeline for the stables. When they arrived, they found the bloody, but still breathing body of the trooper assigned to watch the stables. "S... Sorry Major,I... I let him g...get away," a gasping corporal muttered.

"You did fine, son, just fine," Thurston said. "Did you see which way he went when he rode out."

There was a moment before he gasped, "West Sir, wes...." and he died.

"Sonofabitch," Tye muttered under his breath. "That damn Mexican is gonna pay for this and everything else."

"It's still four hours before daylight. I'll get Garrison and fill him in and you get O'Malley to form a patrol. You can be after him before then." Thurston ordered, his anger and disgust showing in his tone.

◆ VIII ◆

Frank was racing west on the Mail Road as fast as his horse could run. After a couple of miles he stopped and listened for someone following him. He was surprised that he could not hear hoof beats of a lot of horses coming his way. He walked his horse, resting him for the race he was sure would come. He stopped every few minutes to look and listen. He was pleased that no one was chasing him but wondered why.

Unknown by Frank, his passing was noticed by two pair of black eyes belonging to Lone Wolf and Grey Eagle. Lone Wolf came out of the brush and checked the tracks. He was elated when he found the notched one.

He turned to Grey Eagle and said," Go to the camp and get Tanza. Tell him that I, his friend, Lone Wolf, has found the man we search for. I will follow him and to come quickly."

It was very dark with no moon. Lone Wolf had to be careful that he would not accidentally stumble upon the man when he was stopped, which he was doing frequently. Suddenly, he stopped as his pony's ears were twitching. Then Lone Wolfe heard it also, the sound of a walking horse. He moved into the brush only seconds before the man appeared, backtracking. Without thinking, Lone Wolf hurled his body from his mount thru the air and hit the unaware Frank like a battering ram, knocking him from his saddle. Frank hit the ground on his back knocking the wind out of him and Lone Wolf was upon him in an instant and struck him above the ear with the handle of his Bowie, rendering Frank unconscious. Lone Wolfe quickly lifted him, placing him across the saddle. He tied the man's hands together. He then threw the loose end of the rawhide rope under the horse and secured it to the man's feet, holding Frank securely on top of his horse. Lone Wolf mounted his pony, and holding the reins of Frank's horse, led them off the road and headed south. He felt good, and knew his good friend, Tanza, would be pleased.

~

A hour before daylight found Tye leading the patrol out again. There was no grumbling among the men about having to go on patrol this time, in fact many were volunteering. Everyone wanted to get the men responsible for the senseless killing of the escort and the trooper knifed in the stable was popular with everyone. Maybe getting some of their back pay had a little to do with it also. This was another experienced bunch of men that O'Malley hand picked. Men that could be counted on when things got rough. Men that wouldn't be complaining about the heat, lack of water, or short rations. Men that would take orders without question and see that they were carried out. There was no green recruits on this patrol.

Tye found where the scuffle took place and the tracks heading south. He rolled a cigarette and waited for the patrol to catch up. "Looks like we're a little late, Lieutenant." he said, pointing down at the road.

"What do you mean by that?" Garrison asked, trying to figure out what Tye was talking about. All he could see was a bunch of jumbled tracks on the road.

Tye, dismounted as did the Lieutenant. Tye showed him where the horse with the notched shoe had traveled west and then backtracked. He showed him where a body had left an imprint in the soft sand and the moccasin tracks.

"Frank was backtracking probably not believing someone wasn't hot on his heels. An Apache jumped him, knocking him off his horse and probably knocked him out. I figure he's tied to his horse and the Apaches is taking him to meet the main bunch. He then showed the Lieutenant the tracks heading south. After looking for a moment, Garrison could actually plainly see what happened when only moments before he could only see a bunch of tracks that meant nothing. He was quietly pleased with himself but knew he had a lot to learn. Tye was reading what happened just like you would read a page in a book.

With Tye back in front, the patrol headed south following the tracks. Tye had explained to Garrison that he was sure Frank was alive. The Apaches were aware that one of the men involved in killing the Apache boys had a horse with a notched shoe. They were watching the road and checking every passerby's tracks. Frank wasn't dead yet, but if they didn't get to him before the main bunch of Apaches did, he would be wishing he was. The

Apaches had more ways of making a man die a slow and painful death than he could count.

After a couple of hours in the grueling heat, they had covered only three miles. The hard, rocky ground, made tracking a tough business. Tye could find a print here and there and maybe only a scratched rock in between. Sometimes, he lost it completely and had to backtrack. Every wasted minute was letting the Apaches get closer to meeting each other.

It was late afternoon when he felt he was close. A man out here in his profession could feel it when Apaches were near. Some say old so and so could smell'um but he didn't believe that. It was just a feeling that men like himself got.

"Better hold the patrol here, Lieutenant, while I scout ahead. I think we are close and no way this outfit can travel as quiet as one man over this rocky ground."

"Have the men dismount, Sgt., but have them stand by their mounts. We may have to leave in a hurry." Garrison ordered.

Tye had gone less than a mile when he smelled the smoke. He dismounted and made his way to a small rise. He inched his way up it and when he reached the crest, took his hat off peering thru some brush down on the other side.

"Damn," he muttered to himself

On the ground, staked spread eagled was Frank. He was surrounded by twenty or twenty five well armed warriors and in the middle was Tanza himself. Apparently, Frank was unconscious because as he watched, a brave poured water on his face to wake him up. A brave came up to Tanza holding scalps he had probably taken from Frank's saddlebags, causing much shouting and excitement among the rest. Tanza held one of them up and slowly turned to Frank.

"God this ain't going to be pretty," Tye thought to himself, but he was powerless to stop it. Twenty- five to one isn't very good odds. He started to go back down the hill but stopped when he saw Tanza sit straddle of the man's chest. He knew what was coming, and it did. With the experience of taking scalps from many men, the Apache neatly lifted Franks scalp with the precision of a surgeon. He held the bloody mess high for all to see. The Apaches went crazy as their lust for blood and revenge heightened with every passing minute. Tye had to admire Frank for one thing, he didn't let out a scream, only fought the rawhide ropes that bound him. Tye slid down the rise, mounted his horse and quietly rode back to get the patrol.

The scalping was only the beginning of Frank's suffering. Tanza, still sitting on Frank's chest, slid farther down and straddled his thighs. He ripped Frank's shirt off and made a horizontal cut on his chest above his nipples from left to right , just deep enough to bleed. He then did the same about six inches lower and then followed up with several vertical cuts between the two horizontal ones. Using the edge of his knife, he peeled back enough skin to grab hold of and gave a vicious jerk. Frank let out a horrifying scream as the skin was peeled from this body. This was repeated three times, one for each boy he killed. When he passed out from the pain they would pour water on him to wake him up. Lone Wolf, who had left, came back with a sack and poured out a four foot prairie rattler which he had caught.They caught the snake again and while holding its head, tied a rawhide string about two foot from the head and staked it out just out of striking distance of Frank's head. They wet and stretched the rawhide binding that bound his hands and they let some slack in the ones around his feet. As the sun dried the rawhide it would shrink and slowly, painfully slow, pull Frank's head to within striking distance of the rattler. It would bite him time after time resulting in a slow, agonizing death. The Apaches mounted their horses and started to ride off but Tanza had one more indignity for Frank. He raised is rifle and shot him in the crotch. They then rode off yelling and screaming, their bloodlust temporally soothed.

Frank was in such intense pain that the buzzing of the rattler didn't register with his brain. Never had he thought anything could hurt like this. He was praying, asking a God he had forsaken long ago, to help him. When the buzzing finally registered, he slowly turned his head just as the rattler struck. Frank actually saw, for an instant, the open mouth with the fangs extended coming at his face. He screamed in terror and instinctively jerked away. The rawhide holding the rattler kept him from being bitten by a couple of inches. He knew he was a dead man now and braced himself for what was coming.

~

O'Malley had seen Tye coming in a hurry and shouted the order to mount up. They were ready when Tye arrived.

"Did you see the Apaches?" an obviously excited Garrison asked.

"Yes sir, and the Mex, Frank Vasquez. " The Apaches have him prisoner and are doing some brutal things to him   I think we might have a chance to surprise then while they are busy with him."

"Lead the way Mr. Watkins,". Garrison said, trying his best to cover his excitement... or was it fear. He wasn't sure which.

Backtracking quickly, Tye reached where he had left his horse before and dismounting and keeping the patrol here, he climbed the hill to take a look.

He saw no Apaches, only Frank. He waved at the patrol and they headed slightly west, to get around the hill to the other side. O'Malley had given the reins of Tye's horse to another trooper so Tye topped the hill and walked down to Frank. He caught the rattler as the patrol arrived and let it go in the brush. Shooting the rattler would only alert the Apaches of their whereabouts' plus he was taught never to kill a animal except for food. For the time being it was better if the Apaches didn't know they were already being followed. He stuck his hand into Frank's pockets, searching till he found some money.

Garrison dismounted and hurried over to where Frank was. He stopped in his tracks at the sight.

"Merciful God in Heaven," he said and turned away.

Frank, somehow still alive, was mumbling something no one could understand. There were four or five separate bite marks on the neck and side of his head. Flies were thick where his scalp had been lifted. His head was half again it's normal size.

"All of you look at this," Tye ordered as some of the men had turned away from the sight.

"This is what will happen to you if you're not alert out here. .Don't ever, and I'll repeat it again. Don't ever give yourself up to an Apache and expect mercy. He doesn't know the word. It's not even in his language. An Apache respects bravery. If you are captured fighting, you will at least get a quick death. Any sign of weakness, which he can't stand, you will get this," pointing to Frank.

"What are we going to do about him? Can we help him in any way?" Garrison said after recovering from his initial shock.

"Only one way, Lieutenant. Get the patrol mounted and back off." He walked over to Frank and knelt beside him. He took his Bowie and cut the rawhide that bound Frank's right hand.

"Frank, " he said in a low voice, "Frank, can you hear me?"

Frank could only nod his head slightly.

"You know you are done, Frank. Nothing nor nobody can help you now. Do you understand what I'm saying?"

Frank nodded his head and in a barely audible voice whispered. "Kill me."

"I'm going to place a pistol in your hand, Frank. It's cocked, with one bullet. I suggest you put it to good use," Tye said and got up and walked to his horse. He handed Garrison the sizable wad of bills he had taken from Frank.

"There's a lot more in these." O'Malley said handing Garrison Frank's saddle bags. Garrison took the money out and put it with what Tye had taken from Franks pockets.

"Let's go find Tanza. Lieutenant." Tye said and mounted his horse.

"What about Frank?" Garrison asked.

"Frank will take care of Frank, " Tye answered, "When he's ready to."

They rode off with Garrison still wondering what Tye meant. When he heard the shot, he understood.

Tracking Tanza was no problem. Twenty to Twenty-five horses left tracks that a blind man could follow. It didn't take Tye long to figure where they were heading.

" Mexico," he said out loud. He waited for the patrol to catch up.

"Lieutenant, if you want to catch sight of Tanza we're going to have to pick up the pace. He's heading to Mexico," Tye suggested.

"Double time, Sergeant." they headed out at a canter.

The closer they got to the Rio Grande, the more broken the country become. Seldom were they able to travel more than a few hundred yards before a detour around an arroyo was required. Some a few feet deep, others fifty or more. Garrison had never seen a more rugged country, nor one more ruggedly beautiful. He was actually starting to appreciate this land for what it was. How a land like this could harbor such hate and cruelty was beyond his understanding.

"I'm thinking this land is beautiful today and was wondering how anyone could live out here yesterday," he chuckled to himself. His thoughts were interrupted by a loud stream of cuss words coming from Tye.

"The Apaches have swung south, Lieutenant." he said.

"That's good, isn't it. Maybe they aren't going to Mexico," Garrison replied.

"Good Friends of mine, the Turleys, live about four miles south of here. I bet that is where he's headed. His bloodlust is up and it ain't going to stop till he's killed a bunch, or he's killed." Tye wanted to get there quickly but knew that would only ruin the horses. Tanza was a good hour ahead of them and if anything was going to happen at the Turleys, it had already had. They were good people, the Turleys. Jim Turley and Tye's father, Ben, had been good friends. He had a many a good meal there, cooked by Marie Turley. They had a son that was younger than Tye, probably about twenty- four. His wife and two kids, a boy and a girl, all lived on the home place. Good, hard working God fearing family that just wanted to be left alone to live their lives.

"Please Lord, not the Turleys, please." he begged quietly.

The patrol was making good time, considering all the detours being made. Now the mesquite was like a forest causing more detours and worst of all, cutting out any breeze that there was. He could feel the sweat trickling down his back under the buckskin shirt. He knew he smelled to high heaven of tobacco, smoke, and sweat.

"Wouldn't be hard for a Apache that was downwind to smell me coming," he thought to himself. He pulled up suddenly and his heart sank. Black smoke could be seen in the distance... about where the Turley's place was.

◆ IX ◆

As the patrol rode in to the Turley's yard, Tye was heartbroken at what he saw. The house was only half burned as the Apaches were in a hurry and didn't set the fire properly. They did do everything else that a man would expect an Apache to do. Apparently, the Turleys had been caught by complete surprise. Tye dismounted and went to where his friend, Jim was lying. His body was scalped and mutilated. Tye saw Jim's son lying a short distance away, also scalped and mutilated.

"Don't a damn one of you go into that home until I do," he shouted at a startled Lieutenant Garrison as the Lieutenant and two troopers were headed toward the cabin. He then knelt down beside his lifelong friend and tried to say something but the lump in his throat wouldn't allow it. He knelt there for a moment with his back to everyone and then stood up and quickly went into the cabin before they could see his grief. He found what he expected. Both Marie and her daughter- in- law were lying on the floor. Both were stripped and obviously raped, probably by several braves. Their throats had been slashed and both scalped. He couldn't move for a few seconds. His whole body was numb and his mind not functioning at what had happened to this wonderful family that he had cared so much for.

O'Malley's somber voice broke the spell. "What can we do, Tye?"

Tye stood with his back to O'Malley for a few seconds longer, then without turning around quietly said,

"Just bring me a couple of blankets Sarge and keep everyone away from this."

O'Malley returned shortly and handed Tye the blankets.

"Help me out here." Tye said, his hands shaking as he gently lifted the body of Marie so the blanket could be wrapped around her. They did the same to her daughter-in-law.

"Must be the smoke making my eyes water like this," Tye said, trying his best to hide his feelings.

"Yeah, smokes pretty bad in here," O'Malley said wiping his eyes for no reason other than to make Tye feel unalone in his feelings. " Hell, I didn't even know these people and it's almost to much for me,' O'Malley thought to himself.

Tye gathered himself and picked up Marie Turley and carried her outside and laid her beside her husband. O'Malley did the same with the young girl.

Suddenly, Tye remembered the kids. He had been so distraught over Jim and Marie that he had completely forgotten them.

"Lieutenant, there is a four year old little boy and a two or three year old little girl that's not here. Would you have your men look around for them?"

"Certainly, right away," Garrison said and placed his hand on Tye's shoulder, understanding his feelings. He had the patrol in groups of two scouring the area for a hundred yards in all directions. After about twenty minutes, it was obvious that they were missing. "What do you think happened to them, Tye," Garrison asked.

"A lot of times the Apaches will take a young girl and raise her. In two or three years she will be Apache, with no memory of this. A boy, if he shows some spunk, will be taken and adopted by a brave. He will be taught the ways of a warrior. By the same token, if the lad is whimpering and afraid they will usually just kill him right off. An Apache cannot tolerate weakness in a child and certainly not in a grown man. The kids aren't here, so they have taken them. At least they are alive and as long as they are, we have a chance to get them back."

A burial detail was formed and the bodies were given a Christian burial. Garrison read from the Bible and O'Malley led them in a short prayer.

"The Apaches are in Mexico by now, Lieutenant. I suggest we head back to Fort Clark and try to pry some more information from our friends in the guardhouse as to where Alex may be," Tye said. "Tanza will be back and we'll get him then."

The patrol left, headed east, while Tye remained for a few minutes for a last visit with his friends. With everyone gone, he knelt beside his friend's graves and wept unashamedly. He stood up and with his hat in his hand made a promise.

"I swear to you, Jim. I will get yours and Marie's grandchildren back and make that murdering redskin pay for this." He then looked up at the sky and said," Thanks for being my mother and fathers friend and helping me so much after they were gone. I will never forget you."

When he caught up with the patrol and positioned himself beside Garrison, nothing was said for several minutes. The only sound was the horses hooves striking rocks, squeaking saddles, and an occasional cough from one of the troopers. Garrison finally broke the silence.

"Why do they do it, Tye?"

"Why does who do what?" Tye asked, his mind still back yonder with the Turleys.

"What makes people live out here, alone, knowing that can happen at any time?" he asked.

Tye didn't answer for a minute, mulling his answer over in his mind.

"Well, there's men like my father who just didn't like being crowded. He wanted room to do what he wanted to do without someone looking over his shoulder. You have men who want land that they can call their own to do as they please... farm or raise cattle or goats or whatever. Some men just want to see what's over the hill. If it wasn't for men like these, men who wanted these things, we would still be living back east, never venturing toward the west. This land would have no one but Indians living on it.

"I never thought about it like that," Garrison said, scratching the side of his face." I guess we would all be piled up in the cities back East."

"Everyone talks about the men out here, how tough they have to be," Tye continued." No one hardly ever speaks of the women that come with their men. I sometimes think... no, I don't think, I know they have to be as tough or tougher than their men. They have to make a home out of nothing, sometimes just a dugout in the side of a hill. They hardly ever have a chance to talk to another woman on a regular basis, having babies with no doctors, nursing the children and their men with nothing but herbs and home remedies, keeping food on the table without spoiling, having to sometimes fight when their men are gone. You could go on and on about the women out here. They are a special breed, just as their men are."

They were soon back on the Old Mail Road and making much better time than they were. Garrison looked at the country now in a different light than he did a couple days ago. Three weeks ago he was distraught about being assigned out here. Now he was certain of his goal in life... help make this wild, beautiful country safe for people like the Turleys to make a life out here. He felt good. He felt like he was doing something worthwhile for the first time in his young life.

"Yes sir, Major, I'm going to make it out here. You can bet on it," he said to himself.

It was full dark when they saw the lights of Brackettville in the distance.

◆ X ◆

It never ceased to amaze Tye what a transformation was made in the appearance of every patrol he went on when they returned. Even though the troops may be bone tired, hot, and dirty, they would ride into Fort Clark sitting up straight, shoulders square, and to the unknowing, looked like they were on parade. Major Thurston was on the porch, waiting. As they approached, he was at attention and returned Garrison's salute smartly, not the half hearted way he did in his office a couple days ago. He was anxious to get inside and get a report on what had transpired on the patrol. Lt. Garrison dismounted and after shaking the Major's hand, followed him inside.

Tye's attention had been sidetracked. He spotted Rebecca standing off to one side with Mrs. O'Malley. She was waving and even blowing him some kisses. Tye waved back and started to return the kisses but stopped. He thought about what the talk would be if he, the big, bad, tough guy, was seen blowing kisses. He had to laugh at the thought of that. He started toward her when the Major's orderly stopped him, telling him that his presence was required in the Major's office. He stopped, looked at Rebecca, shrugged his shoulders, and motioned to her that he wouldn't be long.

When he entered the office, both Thurston and Garrison were at the wall map.

"Tye, glad the corporal caught you. Come over here and tell me where you think Tanza is and where Alex Vasquez and the rest of his gang could be," the Major said.

Tye walked over to the map, studied it for a moment before saying anything.

"I think both have a camp on the river, both on the Mexican side, somewhere about here," and put his finger just west of where the Turleys place had been.

"If it were me sir, I would have my camp there. It's about the most unapproachable part of the river for several miles due to the many deep canyons and high cliffs along the river. You would have to know the way in and when access to a place is limited, it makes it easier to defend. I think Tanza has a permanent camp there. As far as Alex is concerned, he will be in one of the border towns living it up… on our money. Both of them are feeling pretty damn safe on the Mexican side, Sir."

Thurston stood there for a minute staring at the map. "How many men do you think Alex has left?" he asked.

"Best I can guess, about six or seven," Tye answered.

"We have recovered about twenty-two hundred dollars so far. The faster we can get to them the more of what's left we will recover."

"I don't think they will be in a hurry to come back over here, Major. That's a lot of money anywhere, but it's a whole lot of money over there. It'll take them a while to spend it."

"We have to get them before they do," Thurston said.

Tye and Garrison looked at each other, both thinking the same thing.

"You're not thinking what I think you are, are you, Major? "Tye asked.

The Major let out a sigh, turned and walked to his desk and sat heavily down in his chair. With his hands clasped in front on the desk, he looked up at both of them.

"I," he said then stopped, "No, we, have the responsibility to get that payroll back and punish those responsible for the theft quickly. The troops need their pay. The bandits need to know that a swift and terrible end awaits them if they mess with this man's army. I intend to accomplish both of these points very quickly with the help of both of you."

There was a long silence before the Major spoke again. "I can't order you or any man to do this, but I would like both of you to volunteer and to get a couple more men and cross into Mexico… incognito."

Tye had seen it coming but the idea was a shock to Garrison.

"You mean as a civilian, Sir," he asked with concern written across his face and nervously rubbing the back of his neck.

"Yes, as a civilian. You would carry nothing identifying you as a soldier of the United States Army. Your horse nor your weapons will be army issue. You would be completely on your own with no contact with anyone here in the States. You will be free to take whatever measures you deem necessary to carry out your task."

Tye and Garrison looked at each other, smiled and shrugged their shoulders and then both said they would do it if there was no other way.

A look of relief came over Thurston as he shook both their hands.

"Do I need to explain what it means if you are found out to be United States soldiers, in Mexico... out of uniform. You would be treated as spies and I would have to say you deserted to keep any more hard feelings between the countries than is already there.

"I think we understand, Sir," Garrison said, looking at Tye.

"I would like to have you take more men, but a group of more than three or four men may draw unwanted attention," Thurston said.

Everyone looked at each other not really knowing what to say. Each knew the risk- Garrison and Tye getting tried and shot as spies and Thurston- he would undoubtedly face a highly publicized court-martial. A long awkward minute went silently as each man considered the risk versus the gain. Finally Thurston spoke.

"When can you leave?"

"If you can round up the equipment and horses, including a pack horse, shovels, picks, and supplies, we can leave by noon tomorrow", Tye said.

" Why the pick and shovel?" Garrison asked.

"We need to have a reason for being there and prospecting is as good a reason as any," Tye answered.

"Lieutenant Garrison, you will be in command but you will listen to Tye's advice in all situations before making your decision. Is that clear?" Thurston asked.

"Very clear sir. Does the Major have a idea who else might be included?"

"No. I'll leave that up to you as to who you take. Now, I'm sure you both have a lot to do, so if you'll excuse me I have got to get started getting things together." Thurston said escorting them outside. He shook their hands and turned and went back inside.

Tye rolled a cigarette, lit it, and took a long drag, enjoying the flavor for a moment before saying anything to Garrison. "I'll speak to O'Malley about the other men. You get some rest tonight. I've got a feeling we are in for a long, long patrol."

Tye left him standing there and went to his quarters to freshen up before seeing O'Malley and, of course, Rebecca.

~

It was late when a bathed and shaved Tye knocked on O'Malley's door. The Sergeant answered the door and announced to Rebecca that Tye was here. She came out of her room and rushed over to Tye and hugged his neck and gave him a quick peck on the cheek.

"It took you long enough to get over here," she said, backing up and facing him with her hands on her hips and pretending to be mad.

"It took longer than I expected. Can we all sit down at the table. I've got to talk to Sergeant O'Malley about something that concerns us all."

They all shuffled over to the table, each wondering what was going on. Mrs. O'Malley poured coffee for the men, Rebecca and herself. Rebecca sat nervously rubbing her hands together. She hadn't seen Tye this quiet or subdued, and she could not imagine what was coming but she didn't think it was good.

"Thurston has asked Garrison and me to get a couple of men and cross the river into Mexico to try to apprehend the rest of the Vasquez gang and recover as much of the payroll as possible."

"You can't be serious, Tye. That could lead to some serious political consequences." an astonished O'Malley said.

"I know that. He knows that. We will be going as civilians. Nothing on us that can tie us to the military," Tye said.

Rebecca sat motionless, too stunned by this to even speak. She knew well what could happen. Indians, bandits, and the Federales, would all be possible adversaries. No one over there could help. She was biting her lower lip trying to keep from showing her deep concern.

"Well, when do we leave?" the big Irishman asked.

"Not we, O'Malley, just me. I want you here to take care of things, and looked straight at Rebecca- "things that mean a great deal to me."

O'Malley started to protest, but Tye held up his hand.

"I want you to suggest a couple of men for me to talk to that could handle a long extended expedition and can be counted on in a pinch." Tye said. "Think about it and let me know in the morning who you would suggest.

Right now, if you will allow me, I have another important matter to attend to. He stood up and took Rebecca's small, delicate hands in his large calloused hands. Looking her in the eyes he chewed his lips for a minute steadying himself for what he was going to say.

"Sergeant O'Malley, do I have your permission to ask your niece for her hand in marriage?" he suddenly blurted out.

A gasp came from Rebecca and a shriek of joy came from Mrs. O'Malley, who came rushing over to give both a big hug.

"You sure do my boy," a very happy O'Malley said while patting him on the shoulder. " Come on Ma, let's go for a walk. We've got some planning to do."

"We sure do Pa, wedding plans," she said happily.

Tye looked down at Rebecca and saw she was crying.

"I hope I didn't upset you, honey. I thought it was what you wanted."

"You big dumb gringo," she said laughing. "These are tears of pure happiness. There is nothing I have ever wanted more than for you to ask me to be your wife." She fell against him and swore she would never let him go. They held each other for a long time before Tye turned her face up and gave her a long kiss.

"When," a breathless Rebecca asked.

"As soon as I get back from this job, and when I have the Turley kids back."

She could feel him against her and knew he wanted her as much as she wanted him.

"How about tonight, right now," she said.

Startled, he stepped back and looked at her and realized she was kidding when he saw her laughing. He laughed too.

"Just as soon as I get back, I promise," he said.

"Tye, I don't like you going into Mexico looking for those men. I want you to be here, with me."

"There's nothing I would rather do than spend all of my time with you, Rebecca, but this is something that has to be done. Everything will be alright and I'll be back before you even miss me."

"That will be hard to do since I'll be missing you as soon as you walk out that door," she said as she reached up and put her arms around his neck and pulled his face down for a goodnight kiss.

"Just be careful, darling, and come back to me," she said in a trembling voice, trying to hold back the tears

~

Daylight, as it does most of the time when you are tired, came all too quickly. Tye had met with O'Malley and had gotten two names of men to talk to. He went to see Thurston, and the Major made arrangements for the two men to meet with Tye in an hour. In the meantime, he went to the guardhouse to see Miguel and Jesus. He thought they might have an inkling to give him some information about where Alex may be. The guard let him in with no problem.

"Hey, Miguel, how are you feeling?" he asked when he entered the hall where Miguel and Jesus were. Miguel jumped up and ran over to the window and Jesus cowered in a corner as he did before. Miguel still had slight swelling in his nose and his hand was heavily wrapped and in a sling. The place smelled of urine and sweat.

"Thought one of you boys might tell me where Alex may be right now," Tye said.

Neither one moved or said anything. Tye could tell by the look on their faces that this crazy gringo scared them to death.

"Well," Tye said." If you don't want to volunteer any information, I have to get it another way."

"What you going to do, gringo? Jesus asked, his voice shaking.

"I haven't decided yet but it'll be a lot of fun---for me.Guard!" Tye shouted, "I need to get in one of the cells."

"Okay, okay you crazy gringo. Stay away and I'll tell you what I know," Miguel said in an almost pleading voice.

Tye got the information he wanted, including a crude map. He also told them what had happened to Frank and they were appalled. "If you lied to me." He held up the map. What I will do to you will be worse." He felt he got good information.

The two soldiers were waiting in Thurston's office when Tye was let in by the orderly. Garrison was there also.

"Sorry I'm late, men," he said. "I stopped over at the guardhouse and got some useful info from my two friends over there.

"Tye, this is Del Arnold and Glenn Phipps. We have already discussed everything and they understand perfectly what the situation is and what the consequences could be. They are anxious to go," Thurston said.

Tye shook each of their hands and both had a strong firm handshake and looked Tye straight in the eye. That was good. He never trusted a man who averted looking him eye to eye. "You understand that we are civilians and there will be no yes sir and no sir, no riding side by side as in formation. We will be a very loose, unorganized looking outfit. We are prospectors and that's all we are." They both nodded their understanding.

◆ XI ◆

The supplies Tye requested were ready before noon. By one o'clock the men were looking back over their shoulders at Brackettville. Each man had his own thought as to why he was doing this and what they were leaving behind. None was leaving more than Tye. He had seen her as they rode out. She was waving with one hand and wiping her eyes with the other. It left a lump in his throat and he was glad no one asked him anything right now because he wasn't sure he could speak. Tye rode in the lead and the others were strung out in a loose line behind him. Del was leading the pack horse and Glenn was riding between him and Garrison. The heat was stifling.

'Maybe a little breeze will come up and the wet shirt will feel cool,' Tye thought to himself.

They were traveling west on the Old Mail Road toward Camp Val Verde. They would follow the road for about twenty miles and then veer south- west toward Mexico. It was past noon and no breeze had appeared to help cool things down. The men, except for Tye, were riding as if half asleep. Tye was keeping his eyes moving. He learned a long time ago that the quickest to doze off was to get your eyes set on something for a period of time. If you kept them moving all the time the drowsiness didn't seem to come as quickly. Some dust in the distance caught his eye, and he blinked the sweat out and looked again.

"Just a little old whirlwind," he said patting his horse. This time of year they were plentiful but always caused Tye to be apprehensive when he spotted one.

Garrison pulled up beside him.

"Been wondering about something, Tye. " he said.

"What's that?"

" In ten patrols how many would you figure you would actually see action against the Apache?" he asked.

Tye thought before answering. "Maybe two or three," he said. "Why?"

"This is my third and I haven't seen one yet, unless you count those dead boys." he said.

"There's an old saying," Tye said, "The days were long, the men were riding with dry throats. The Indians didn't beat them, the land did. Thirst, hunger, boredom, and the frustration of not being able to face your enemy, whips the army out here. The Indians know it too.. They know we will pursue them for a ways but always quit because of hunger or thirst. The Indians aren't stupid. They know they cannot face the army in a face- to- face confrontation. They don't have the firepower or the numbers. So, they fight smart. Hit here, hit there, do what damage they can do and get the hell away as fast as they can. Pursue them too fast, not paying attention, you could get yourself ambushed. An ambush is what you have to fear and the Apache is a master of this because of his patience. That's where you can lose a lot of men in a hurry, not in a face- to- face fight."

Tye pulled up suddenly and Garrison's horse almost bumped into his.

"What is it?" Garrison asked. "What did you see?"

"Dunno," Tye answered. "Just some movement out of the corner of my eye on that hill over there." He was pointing with his rifle which he had already jerked out of its scabbard out of habit. They watched for a full minute.

"Whatever it was has dropped behind that second hill," Tye said.

Even as he spoke, a few antelope came from behind the hill.

"Just some antelope," Tye said as he slid the rifle back in the saddle scabbard.

"Never hurts to play it safe. Could just have just as easy been Apaches or bandits." he said.

'I've a hell of lot to learn,' Garrison was thinking. 'Thurston was right when he said Tye could teach me things if I would listen. He practically had to point the damn antelope out before I saw them. How he seen them earlier I'll never know. I've got just about all the book learning a man can get and here I am, a student to a man who has never sit in a classroom.' He smiled at the thought.

He thought about that for a minute. 'That's not exactly true either.' Garrison looked around at this vast land, 'He's been in a classroom every day of his life. You just don't get a's or b's out here... you get life or death.'

They turned southwest before dusk and made a camp about three miles from the Old Mail Road.

"No fires after dark," Tye said." No use advertising where we are."

He wanted to learn a little about the two men that were with them. Garrison hadn't been here long enough to know them. They had been on some of the patrols that Tye had led but he didn't know them other than recognition of their faces. He would visit with each after they all had eaten. Besides, sitting around drinking coffee naturally leads to a lot of talk. Their sparse meal consisted of cold biscuits dipped in bacon grease and hot bacon. After eating their fill, Tye put more coffee on the coals to boil.

"Damn tin cup," Arnold said patting his lips with his fingers, "It done melted my lips together," bringing a round of laughter from everyone.

"I've been on how many patrols with you, Del, ten or twelve? You burned your lips on every damn one of them. I swear you ain't got a brain in that big noggin' of yours," Phipps said laughing.

"If we are going to talk about smarts, Mr. Phipps, why don't you tell them about your forgetting to tighten your saddle girth and busting your ass when it slipped sideways on the last patrol?" Arnold replied.

The vision of Phipps sprawled on the ground with the slipped saddle brought a new round of guffaws from everyone. Tye liked them both.

"What prompted you to join the cavalry, Arnold?" Tye asked.

"Well," he paused scratching the back of his neck, "Reckon its a pretty common story of a lot of other men in the army. I got in a little trouble with the law and enlisting seemed a way out."

"What kind of trouble?" a concerned Tye asked. He didn't want any thieves in this outfit seeing they may have their hands on a lot of money.

"Seems this lady I was seeing failed to tell me she was married, and her husband happened in at a very inconvenient moment and wasn't in a very understanding mood. It was him or me--- he lost. Weren't my fault, but the local law didn't approve of me killing one of their citizens. That was about nine years ago. Been soldiering ever since."

"Was she worth it," Garrison asked?

"Damn right she was," Arnold said without hesitation, cracking everyone up.

Tye got up and filled his and everyone else's cup with the last of the hot coffee.

"What about you, Phipps, why did you get in?" he asked.

"Seemed like the thing to do at the time. My pa and maw and me had a piece of land we were farming back in Georgia. Just a small piece, you understand. We weren't no slave owners or anything like that. Some men rode in one day while I was in town getting supplies. When I got back, both maw and pa were dead and the place was on fire. I buried them on the place, sold what I could salvage, paid their bill at the store and started moving on. Ended up broke and hungry so I joined the army. Found out in the army, everyone was broke but not always hungry," he said chuckling to himself.

"Ain't it the damn truth," Arnold added laughing.

The coals had burned down and it was full dark when everyone rolled up in their bedrolls to get some sleep. Tye made one round of the camp, checked the horses, making sure they were secure. He rolled up and was immediately asleep knowing there was no better sentries than the horses.

~

It was mid morning and they had been moving since before daylight. There was actually a low cloud cover and the temperature was comfortable for a change. They were close to the Rio Grande now and the land had suddenly changed. Instead of low rolling hills, there were now deep arroyos, and canyons that caused a constant change of direction, even backtracking sometimes, to get around them. The land had a very short grass covering it where there wasn't rocks. Cactus was growing everywhere, even in the cracks of some of the larger rocks. There was a lot of sage and cedar. The chaparral, or mesquite, was a little more sparse here than where they had come from. It was a land that possessed a natural, rugged beauty.

"If Miguel didn't lie we should be cutting an old buffalo trail pretty soon that heads toward the river." Tye stated.

It was a common practice out here that to find water, or a easier trail, you found an old buffalo or game trail and followed it. The animals would always find the easiest path to where they were going. The trick was to figure out which direction the animals were heading for water if their tracks were wiped out by wind, rain, or in a lot of instances, hadn't been used for awhile.

It was past noon when they stopped for a break. Tye left them to scout ahead while they took a breather. It didn't take him long to find the river and what looked like a camp on the other side, Mexico side.

"Damn if Miguel didn't tell the truth, ole friend," he said speaking to his horse. He sat there a few minutes and rolled a smoke while studying the camp.

"That's one hell of a spot for a camp," he mused. He was looking at the high cliffs behind the camp when he spotted the spring that was gushing from the sheer wall forming what looked to be a deep pool before flowing into the river. The river was too deep and swift here for a safe crossing. The camp was in a great defensive position. There was plenty of cover if someone was attacking them from across the river and the high cliff had a overhang that would prevent anyone shooting at them from above. It looked like there were only two ways in to the camp.

Tye figured they would have to go downstream a ways to get across and come back to the camp. To go downstream instead of upstream was a good decision but he wasn't aware of it. About four miles upstream was the camp of Tanza and his bunch of renegades and by going upstream he would surely have stumbled onto them. His little group would not have had a chance against twenty-five or so Apaches.

The others in his group were waiting for him when he got back. He explained what he found and that they were going to have to go downstream to find a crossing. They retraced Tye's path to the river and then headed south. Tye found out immediately this wasn't going to be a easy task. The arroyos were plentiful and deep. Once they had to swing two miles out of the way to find a way to cross to the other side of one of them. It was well past mid afternoon when they found a place to cross the river. From the tracks, it looked like everyone in the country used it. The water only reached the horse's bellies and wasn't swift enough to be a problem, and the crossing was uneventful.

"We're in Mexico now," Tye said. "Remember, we are prospecting, and make damn sure if we are questioned, no army lingo comes out in your conversation with them."

They started back up stream toward the camp that Tye had found earlier. The going was easier on this side than on the Texas side and they arrived at the camp shortly before dusk. Everyone, like Tye had been, was impressed with the camp. Even Garrison, with his lack of experience, commented on the good points.

"Get a fire started and the cooking done before its full dark," Tye said.

He walked over to the spring coming out of the cliff and when cupping his hands to get a drink was shocked as to the good taste and to how cold it was. He figured this water was coming from real deep in the bowels of the earth. It was colder than Los Moras Springs back at the Fort, but was no where close in the volume of water produced. The pool looked about four foot deep and was crystal clear. Looking up he could not see the sky because of the overhand high above him.

"Just like I thought, no one can shoot you from above if you stay close to the canyon wall."

He made a complete round of the camp and finally figured which direction the men had rode off in. Hopefully, it was the Vasquez bunch. The smell of bacon and coffee greeted him when he returned to the men. It was full dark when they finished eating and drinking the coffee. The fire had been put out and it was dark, damn dark. The clouds had moved on and the stars shown like lanterns above them. Their eyes slowly adjusted to the darkness and they could see well enough to move around some and get their bedrolls spread out.

"Did you find what direction the bunch that were here went," Arnold asked Tye.

"Yeah," Tye answered. "This place only has two ways in and out so it wasn't hard to find their tracks.

"Well, I'll tell you one thing," Phipps said, "I'm going to remember this place. It would be a hell of a place to build a cabin."

"I was thinking the same thing," Garrison added.

"The first time it comes one of those big rains up stream, Del and I will come down and find your drowned carcasses and give you a Christian burial, "Tye said laughing.

"What do you mean by that?" a bewildered looking Garrison asked.

"You ever hear of a flash flood before?" Arnold asked. "I've seen places like this have a twenty or thirty foot wall of water come downstream and never rained within twenty miles of where I was."

After more small talk, each man drifted off to sleep. All except Garrison. He lay there for awhile wondering if it was raining anywhere upstream.

✦ XII ✦

The eastern sky was just turning gray when the little group moved out of the camp following the tracks the men had left.

"How many do you figure?" Garrison asked.

"Same as before, about six or seven, "Tye replied. "Ground's too hard and rocky to tell exactly."

"How much of a head start you figure they have?"

"Twenty four hours at the least, maybe a day and a half at the most."

Thick mesquite, huge boulders, cliffs, and arroyos made travel difficult and slow. Tracks could be found only occasionally on the rocky ground. Garrison was learning fast. At first he could not see the tracks that Tye was following and Tye would have to point them out. Sometimes it was a track, other times a turned over rock, horse hair on a mesquite thorn, or maybe a broken mesquite limb. By midmorning they were out of the canyons and arroyos and into rolling hills. The tall mountains could be see in the not too far distance. If one didn't know better, he would think he was still in Texas. The mesquite, cactus, and the rocky land looked the same. About noon they saw the adobe buildings in the distance and Tye pulled up. He led them into a stand of tall mesquite about fifty yards off the trail.

"No use anyone seeing us all together," Tye said. Arnold and I will go in and scout around. Miguel back at the Fort gave me a good description of Alex and one called Felipe. We will be back in a couple of hours. Garrison, you and Phipps stay out of sight till we return."

When Tye and Arnold left, Garrison and Phipps moved deeper into the thick mesquite, dismounted, loosened their mount's saddle girths, and sat down in the shade of a particularly large mesquite to wait. On the way into the small village Tye was giving Arnold the description Miguel had given him.

"Alex is built like a stump. Not very tall but heavy thru the shoulders and has a scar on his right cheek. Felipe is in his forties, the oldest of the gang, and is very thin. He always wears a sombrero with a black band with silver coins around the crown. He is one to watch. He is as ruthless as Alex."

They barely got a glance from the Mexicans on the street as they rode in. It had been awhile since Tye had seen poverty like this- kids running around half naked and filthy, men sitting idly in the shade doing nothing. They dismounted in front of the cantina and, after tying their horses to the rail, removed their saddlebags and rifles.

"No use tempting anyone by leaving anything out here," Tye said as they entered the cantina.

It was dark inside and much cooler than outside. They stood just inside the door letting their eyes adjust to the dim light. There were several Mexicans inside sitting at the tables. Tye and Arnold sat down at one of the empty tables in the corner, backs against the wall. Tye noticed that no one was paying much attention to them except two men at one of the tables against the far wall. They were staring and whispering to each other when suddenly, one got up and went outside. Tye got up and casually walked to the bar and ordered two beers and turning around, looked through the door outside. The Mexican was looking at their horses and saddles. Tye walked back to the table and sat down with Arnold and just as he put the mug to his lips the one outside came back in. He walked over to the table he had gotten up from and said something to the Mexican still sitting there and shook his head 'no'. He looked over his shoulder at Tye and sat back down.

"This damn beer is warm and it taste like piss." Arnold said spitting the beer out on the floor.

"Don't drink it then" Tye said," But we're not leaving till our friends over there do. I think they are too interested in us . Either they plan to try to rob us later or they are watching for gringos following them.

"You think they're part of the bunch we're after?" Del asked.

"I'd bet my life on it. They look out of place here, just like we do."

The two Mexicans got up and went outside and walked down the street.

"You want we should get them now?" Del asked.

"No, if they are part of the bunch, I want them to lead us to Alex and the rest."

Tye got up and walked to the door and, without exposing himself, looked down the street where the two were mounting their horses when a third one came out of one of the adobe houses. A tall, thin, Mexican wearing a sombrero with a black belt with some shiny objects on it around the crown. The three were talking and looking at the cantina. Tye slipped further back in the darkness of the room.

"The tall one is Felipe", he said to himself. "They are part of the Vasquez gang after all."

Tyes mind was racing now, trying to figure out the next step when he realized he wasn't going to have to, because they were heading back to the cantina. He hurried back over to the table and sat down, drawing his gun and holding it in his lap under the table. He hurriedly told Del what was happening. Del laid his rifle on the table, pointing the barrel toward the door, resting his hand close and ready.

The three walked in and looked straight at Tye and Del for a couple seconds, then when they could see better, walked back to the table they were at before and sat down. They moved the chairs to where none of their backs were completely toward the gringos.

"What you think, Tye?"

"We'll sit here and see what happens. Just be ready for anything," Tye replied.

Tye noticed Del moved his hand down and wiped his palms. He was obviously nervous. Tye was showing no outward emotion but was churning inside. He wasn't nervous that he was fixing to be in a gun fight but nervous from not knowing what was coming. He sat there, his right hand holding the pistol and his left hand on the table, his fingers unconsciously drumming out an unknown tune on the table. He was thinking three of them and two of us. One of us is probably going to be hit if its comes to a gunfight. He only hoped it wasn't a killing hit. He continued staring at the three Mexicans who were arguing among themselves about something.

Del was staring at the three also but he wasn't missing the way Tye was acting when a fight to the death was fixing to happen.

'I'm about to dirty my pants and this guy's acting like he's calm as can be waiting on a meal to be brought to him,' Del thought to himself.

Suddenly, the tall one stood up and looking straight at Tye, walked outside. The remaining two sat there and finished their drinks and then got up and slowly made their way to the door also.

A relieved Del nervously asked Tye, "What the hell is happening. They know, or at least think they know, who we are."

"I'm not sure but I don't think it would be wise for either of us to walk out that door right now." Tye answered.

"You think they are waiting to ambush us?" he asked.

"Sure as God made little green apples," Tye replied.

"Then how do you figure we're getting the hell outa here," Del asked excitedly.

"First thing is to calm down," Tye said giving Del a smile. "There is probably a back door so wait here a minute."

Tye stood up and walked to the back of the cantina and found the door. He opened in half way and took a long look around until he was satisfied that no one was waiting back there. He closed the door and walked back to Del and sat down.

"There's a door like I figured. It's used to go to the outhouse."

"What are we going to do?" Arnold asked.

"We're gonna do nothing for awhile. Let them wonder what we're doing."

They sat there for a long thirty minutes. It was the longest thirty minutes in Del's life. He had been in skirmishes before and was good in a fight but those skirmishes were always happening unexpectedly and usually over in a few minutes. This waiting, knowing it was going to happen, was for the damn birds.

"I'm going to ease out the back door and see if I can find them. You go over to the door but don't expose yourself. If I find them, there will be some gunfire and it will divert them long enough for you to take up a position across the street… if you don't hesitate."

Tye walked to the back, and opened the door and eased outside, trying to stay in the shadows.

"Damn smell would choke a horse'" he thought. The wall opposite him was used as a urinal for men too lazy to walk to the outhouse which was some fifty yards away. He rounded the corner and walked about fifty yards, staying close to the walls and sprinting between the houses. When he figured he was far enough, he walked between two of them to the street. Looking around the corner, he surveyed the street. It was obvious that everyone knew something was going to happen, as there were no kids playing like there were an hour earlier. The men that had been sitting on the porches were no where to be seen. He did spot one of the men who was crouched behind a barrel about forty feet from where Tye stood. His back was toward Tye.

"Wished I still had my moccasin boots on instead of these damn leather soled boots. I could injun up behind him and cold cock him before he knew I was there. Now, one of us is going to die. There was no way he was going to back shoot any man. He would have to give him a chance to give up. He looked one more time for the others before saying.

"Hey hombre, you looking for me?"

He saw the man stiffen as he spoke and thought he was going to give himself up when the Mexican rolled to one side and came up with his rifle. Tye fired an instant before the Mexican and his quick shot was accurate. He had aimed for the chest but was a little low and the man took the bullet in the stomach. The Mexican's shot went harmlessly into the dirt. Tye seen Del sprinting across the street without a shot being fired so he figured his ruse worked. He walked to where the man lay doubled over, moaning but all the time his eyes were searching the street for the others. It was then that he heard the horses, at least two, heading away from town. He got to the man and pulled his pistol from his scabbard and threw it away and kicked his rifle away from him. He knelt down and saw the man wasn't going to make it. A gut shot was usually fatal and it was a slow, painful death.

"You speak English?" Tye asked.

The man shook his head no and spoke in Spanish. Tye knew enough to know what he was saying wasn't nice. His eyes showed a lot of pain. He was still cussing Tye in Spanish when Tye stood up and hollered at Del to come over. When Del got there he looked down and saw the Mex was done for.

"You think that was the other two that I heard riding off.?"

"Yeah," Tye answered. " This ones done for."

"Has he said anything," Del asked.

"Only questioning who my mother was and several other insults to me in Spanish. He's a tough hombre, I'll say that for him."

The man's eyes were starting to dim and his breathing was getting shallow. Tye reached in the dying man's shirt pocket and pulled out a wad of bills. A rough count came to five hundred and seventy- five dollars.

"Won't be long now." Del said looking at the money. "That's more money than I have ever seen at one time in my life.

"I wonder if he thinks it was worth it?" Tye said. "Get the horses and bring them here and we'll take a look to see what exact direction they left in."

By the time Del returned with the horses, the Mexican was meeting his maker. A sparse crowd had gathered and were pointing and jabbering to each other. Tye and Del rode between the buildings and toward where they had heard the horses running. The tracks were easy to pickup and Tye suggested Del go get Garrison and Phipps. He was going to follow the tracks and they were to follow him when they returned. He would wait on the trail somewhere for them to catch up.

Running horses leave a trail a blind man could follow but Tye knew this would change in a mile or so. The land here was gently rolling hills but he could see the higher ones a short distance ahead.

'Sure glad it ain't like the land around the river,' Tye was thinking. 'The way this land lays, it'll be hard to lay up and ambush someone unless its a long shot with a sharps 50 cal. rifle. Don't believe either one of them will have one of those old buffalo guns.' He came to where the horses slowed some and then down to a walk and the trail immediately got harder to follow on the rocky ground.

It was slow going as sometimes the trail just disappeared. At times when it did, Tye would have to stop and try to figure what direction they went. At those times he did what his pa had taught him. He would put himself in the person's place he was tracking . Every time so far he had guessed right and had managed to pick up the trail again. He was leaving enough tracks and marks for Garrison to follow him. It was hot and he probably needed to rest his horse so he decided to wait for the others in the shade of a large mesquite. He poured some water in his hat and gave the horse a drink and then he loosened the girth and let him graze on the short, sparse grass. Tye laid down on his side in the shade and propped himself on one elbow, chewing a piece of grass, waiting.

~

Felipe and his partner rode into Alex's camp at dusk. He told Alex about the two gringo's and about the shoot-out.

"How come you did not try to kill this man? Alex demanded his temper rising.

" If we had gotten ourselves shot you would not have known about these men and they would have surprised you somewhere on the trail or in town" Felipe said.

"Perhaps," Alex said. "Maybe you did the right thing. Do you think this gringo was Tye Watkins?"

"Could have been. He was tall and big shouldered like you described a few days ago to Frank. Not that many men that tall out here."

"If it was him, he will follow you here. We will leave early in the morning and somewhere on the trail, before the next town, I will have a surprise for him." Alex said smiling.

◆ XIII ◆

It was almost dark when Tye saw his men in the distance. He stood up where they could see him and waved. They saw him immediately and headed his way in a hurry.

"Sure glad to see you, Tye, " Garrison said. "We're not much at tracking even though you were doing your best to make it easy," he said.

"I was getting a little worried about you boys since it was getting close to dark. I sure wouldn't want you boys to have to spend the night by yourselves out here," Tye said laughing. He mounted his horse and pointed to a spot about a hundred yards away.

"There's a small wash over there where we can build a fire without it being seen. After eating we'll move up on the side of the hill to sleep. Maybe we can get a breeze and make it a little cooler." It wasn't long before the smell of coffee and bacon frying filled the air. They had something extra tonight. Del had snuck some potatoes out of the mess hall and had been saving them. He sliced them up and fried them in the bacon grease. Out here, it was a feast to enjoy.

It was going to be a full moon tonight but right now it was quite dark as they prepared their bedrolls.

"I'm sure that Alex knows we are back here by now. I think it would be smart to set up a watch tonight," Tye said. "I'll take the first watch. Garrison, you take the second, then Del and Phipps. Phipps, when your watch is up, get me and I'll stand the last watch. I really don't think tonight he'll try anything, but don't get careless. We can't leave as early as we normally do cause tracking is hard enough in these rocks in the daytime and would be impossible in the dark."

Tye took his rifle and walked off a ways to settle in for his watch.

"Hey Del, I ain't had a chance to ask you what happened in the village," Phipps said.

"Well, we pretty well knew they knew who we were. At first we didn't know for sure who they were. When Felipe showed up, Tye was sure. After that we knew there was going to be a fight and someone, or more than one, was going to be killed. I don't mind telling you I was scared. My palms were sweating and it seemed like I couldn't get enough air. I've been in fights before but this was different, just waiting, knowing it was going to happen."

"How did Tye handle it? Garrison asked quietly not wanting Tye to overhear.

"Hell," Del said." That guy has ice water in his veins. He just sat there strumming his fingers to some tune on the table and waited. When the time came, he wasn't hesitant for a second on what he needed to do. He did it too."

Tye was about thirty yards away sitting against a rock where he would not be silhouetted against the sky. He could hear the horses munching their oats that had been put out by Phipps. The only other sound was a distant coyote, his eerie howling piercing the night air as he howled at the moon which was just breaking over the tops of the hills. This was always the worse time to be on watch, and was why he wanted the first one. He's saw it many times…the shadows from the light of the rising moon would cause shadows to creep across the ground. Shadows from boulders, mesquites, and the tall yucca plants would make it a little nervous for one not use to it. A full moon would make it hard for anyone to sneak up on them. He was drinking some of the strong coffee and listening, watching, and staying alert. By the time his first watch was over, the moon was full and you could see quite easily. He shook Garrison awake and gave him a cup of coffee.

"Find you a place and sit. Don't get silhouetted against the sky. It's light enough for a man to be fairly accurate with a rifle. When your watch is up, tell Del the same thing and tell him to tell Phipps."

Garrison stretched and yawned before getting up. Taking the coffee he walked to the spot Tye had used and sat down to do his watch. The night passed uneventful and with the gray streaks of dawn they were on the trail again.

"How close do you figure we are to them?' Garrison asked.

"Close enough to keep a sharp eye out for an ambush. They know we're following, and Alex is not dumb. He'll leave a man or two at different spots to try and take care of us."

It was only two hours later when they found where the Mexicans had camped. Not wasting time, Tye found their tracks and they were off again. Tye had all his senses working, his eyes taking in every detail, his ears being sensitive to every sound. This trail was too plain, almost like they were going out of their way to make it easy to follow. This worried him a lot and he was searching the distant hills and shrubs for a rifleman. He pulled up suddenly and pointed to the ground.

"They stopped here for some reason, and if I was a betting man, it would be for Alex to get a man or two hid somewhere for a ambush. But where?" His eyes was scanning the horizon when he saw it. On the side of a hill about a quarter of a mile ahead there was a cluster of huge boulders. They would provide plenty of hiding places. It was the only place he could see that would offer a hiding place.

"Ya'll take a break while I backtrack and then come around behind that hill and take a look what's there."

"You see something up there or what?" Garrison asked.

"Just a feeling I get every once in a while," Tye answered as he rode off back down the trail.

He went far enough to where he could not see the boulders and turned off the trail to come up behind the hill. He rode carefully, not sure that they were there or in another spot. Hell, he could be in one of their sights now. He worked his way down and out of an arroyo and stopped to look and listen. His best guess put him behind the hill that the boulders were on so he dismounted, made his way slowly and very carefully to the top. Taking his hat off he looked down the other side and saw he had guessed right. The boulders were right in front of him and so were two horses. He hadn't located the men yet but at least he knew he had been right and if they had ridden much farther one or two of us would have been shot. He eased over the top of the hill and worked his way down to the boulders.

He got to the horses but still no sign of the men. He untied the horses and slapped them on the rear with his rifle and started them running. He threw himself against the nearest boulder and waited. A loud string of Spanish obscenities were coming from inside the cluster of boulders. One man burst out suddenly and almost ran into Tye who clipped him on the chin with the butt of his rifle, knocking him out cold. A yell came from behind him and he threw himself to the right just as a bullet whipped by his head. Turning in midair, he fired at the Mexican. He knew he had missed as soon as he fired but his shot was close enough that the Mexican missed his hurried second shot. Tye hit the ground hard on his back, stunning him for a second. The Mexican was fixing to put an end to this gringo when a barrage of shots from below drove him to the ground . That gave Tye enough time to aim and fire. His bullet caught the Mexican high in the forehead and exploded out the back of his head splattering blood, bone fragments, and brains all over the rocks. Tye got to his feet and walked over to the unconscious Mexican and sat down to wait on the others.

"You okay?" a concerned Garrison asked when they arrived.

"Yeah, thanks to you firing those shots that distracted him for a second."

"Go thru his pockets and see if he has any of the payroll on him,' Garrison said, nodding to Arnold. " Phipps, let's you and me see what we can do with the one Tye cold- cocked." Tye climbed back up the hill and down the other side to retrieve his mount.

"How in hell do you figure he knew they were up there? Phipps asked.

"Don't get me to lying." Garrison said, "But I'm glad he's on our side. Its like O'Malley told me the other day when he was talking about Tye. There's none better at what he does. I swear, he's made a believer out of me."

They went thru the Mexicans pockets until they found the money, roughly five hundred dollars. They tied him up and waited for Tye to return. In the meantime, Phipps brought the money that he had found on the dead Mexican to Garrison. There was four hundred and sixty dollars in his pockets. Tye returned and they gathered around him and waited his instructions.

"Has the other Mex came to yet?"Tye asked.

"He's starting to moan and groan some Tye. I think you shattered his jaw," Del said.

""We can't leave him here, so throw some water on him to wake him up and tie him to his saddle. We need to cover a lot more ground today, so lets go."

They were on the trail again in a very few minutes. The Mexican was swaying in his saddle and doing a lot of groaning and complaining.

"How do you say shut-up in Spanish?" Del asked.

"Dunno." Phipps answered. "But if you threatened to smash him in that busted chin in English, I bet he will get the idea."

They were traveling at a good clip since apparently the trail that Tye was reading was pretty plain. They had gone about four miles from the ambush site when Tye pulled up suddenly.

"Dammit, "They split into two groups," he said as he pointed to the tracks. He sat there for a moment and said" We can't split up, so we'll have to decide which one to follow."

They all looked at each other and Garrison spoke for all three of them.

"You pick one, Tye. We'll follow."

Tye leaned forward and put his hands on the pommel on his saddle and thought for a minute. He decided on staying with the trail they were on. He thought maybe Alex sent two men the other way to draw us off him. That's what I would do if I was as sorry a piece of horse dung as he was. That would be like Alex, to maybe let two of his men die so he could get away.. Also, there were three men on this trail, he figured Alex was one of them. Again they were making no concerned effort to hide their trail.

They were getting deeper into Mexico, closer to the mountains. The terrain was getting more uneven with sharp rising hills, and lots of arroyos and small canyons. A thousand places for a ambush. The hair was standing on the back of Tyes neck. He fully expected a bullet at any second. His eyes were searching every possible hiding place as well as following the tracks. He damn near jumped from his horse once when a rabbit jumped up in front of them.

"Damn, Tye, settle down. You've done this a hundred times trailing Apaches and Alex is no Apache. Just relax," he was telling himself. "You stay uptight and your going to get yourself killed and everyone with you. Maybe it's because in Texas I know the land as well as those I'm hunting. I don't have a clue what's around the next hill here and Alex does."

He pulled up and searched the terrain ahead, not missing anyplace a man could hide. Turning in the saddle he said. "Bring the Mexican up here."

When he was up front Tye put his hat on the Mexican and the Mexicans hat on himself.

The man was about half out of it but would serve Tye's purpose. If he lived he was a dead man anyway cause he would hang. He might just draw enough attention that I can spot them before they open up. He started the men up again with one change, the Mexican was in front with Tye's hat on and on Tye's horse. The tracks were pretty fresh now, probably less than two hours old. If anything was going to happen he figured it would be soon. There was just to many places a man could hide.

Ten minutes later the Mexican's head exploded and a second later the crack of the rifle reached them. Each man hit the ground holding onto their horse's reins and crawling toward a large boulder for cover.

"What the hell happened?" Garrison asked.

"You knew that was going to happen didn't you?" Arnold shouted excitedly. "That's the reason you put your hat on that Mexican and put him up front ain't it."

Tye didn't answer. He was trying to figure out where the shot came from. The Mexican was knocked straight backwards from his horse so the shot came from the front. He was concentrating on a brush pile just left of the trail they were on. It wasn't thick enough to completely stop a bullet but thick enough to hide a man. That's the only spot in front a man could be hiding within rifle range that he could see.

"All of you see the brush pile to the left of the trail?" They nodded their heads. "When I fire, I want each of you to start firing into that pile until I say quit."

He took careful aim for the center of the pile and fired. All hell broke loose as the others opened up with their single shot rifles and then with their side arms. Branches and splinters of wood was flying in all directions from the pile.. Tye signaled a stop to the firing and everything seemed strangely quiet after so much noise. He watched for a moment and then stood up and mounted his horse. The others followed suit. When they got to the brush pile they found another Mexican, dead, riddled with bullets. Tye dismounted and pulled some bloody bills out of the mans pocket.

"This money is getting more and more expensive to those who have it," Tye said. The others nodded in agreement. They also knew that Tye was something special, and each man knew he would never doubt anything he asked them to do. He just had a sense for smelling out danger and avoiding it, and taking care of it as in this case.

Garrison was believing every story he had heard about Tye. In fact, he was going to start a few more if they lived thru this.

"We're slowly cutting them down to where we are even," Tye said. " Unless he picks up more men, I think he is down to himself and no more than four men. If I have been reading sign right, I'd say three." We just made enough noise to wake the dead and if anyone was near enough to hear, they are probably coming to investigate so lets get moving. I know they have to be patrols of Mexican soldiers around here and I don't care to answer questions… do you?"

◆ XIV ◆

Tanza was feeling invincible right now while sitting in his wickiup at the camp on the Rio Grande. He had taken scalps, stole several horses, had four captive children, and avenged his brother's death. All this and he had not lost a man. The men with him believed him to have strong medicine and the Great Spirit was watching over them.. A few more successful raids and the other young warriors would come to him like bees to honey. Every brave with him had rifles and some had revolvers also. As usual though they were short on ammunition but he would fix that with a couple more raids.

He hated the white man as much as he hated the Mexicans. The whites wanted their land and the Mexicans had bounties on Apache scalps for a long time. They didn't care if the scalps were man, woman, or child. They just wanted dead Apaches. The white man wanted their land and had made several promises to do this or that for the Apache for the land. They lied. All white men were liars and he would never trust one again. He would live like an Apache warrior should live and he would die as an Apache warrior should…fighting his enemies. A couple of more days and it would be time…time to cross the river again and kill more white eyes.

~

Arnold and Phipps had covered the dead Mexican with rocks before they hit the trail again. They still had about two hours of daylight left and Tye wanted to put some distance between themselves and the dead Mexicans. The terrain had begun to be more and more inhospitable. The hills were becoming steeper and much more rocky. The only thing growing were the cactus, yucca, prickly pear plants and the ever present sage. The mesquite and grass were left behind as they moved deeper into the mountains. Tracking was next to impossible on the rocky ground. Tye could find a scratch on the rocks made by a shoe every so often but that was all. The only good thing was that it wasn't that important anymore. The terrain made it impossible to go but one way. The main worry Tye had was that by finding very few tracks it kept him from knowing how far behind they were. They could stumble upon them accidentally and that could lead to a disaster. If you were moving, you were at a disadvantage up here because the steel horse shoes striking the rocks wasn't exactly quiet. Anyone within a quarter of mile could hear them coming and set up all kinds on interesting welcomes.

It was hotter than hell. The slight breeze felt like it was coming from an oven, and the late afternoon sun reflecting off the rocks didn't help. Their throats were parched as Tye was making them ration their water carefully. He didn't know when they would find water again. It was harder on the horses than the men and

Tye knew they were in trouble if they didn't find water pretty soon. His eyes were searching for three things now, tracks,trouble, and signs of water.

He called for a halt and everyone dismounted and loosen their saddle girths. Each man poured a little water in his hat and gave their horse a drink and Tye also gave the pack horse some of his. The sun was falling behind the cliffs and was offering a little shade and respite from the heat.

"I'm walking ahead a ways and see what's up there," Tye said. "Y'all just relax a few minutes."

Tye was getting worried now, more for dying of thirst than of bullets. All the men's lips were cracked and even putting pebbles in his mouth had failed to put moisture in his mouth. Somewhere there had to be water. He had seen lots of deer droppings and they sure as hell couldn't live without it. He was about a half a mile ahead when he came across it, a trail that obviously been used for years by the animals just by judging the depth of it. He turned around and went back to get the his men and horses

"Have any luck finding water?" Phipps asked hopefully.

"Maybe,"Tye answered. "Lets walk our horses while we take a look"

Tye was watching his horse closely as they walked toward the game trail. When they were close his horses head came up and his ears pricked forward.

"Thank God," Tye said "He smells the water." He looked back and the other horses were doing the same and he could see grins on Arnolds and Phipps faces. Garrison was too green to know what the horses acting like that meant.

"What the hell are you three grinning about?" he asked.

"You'll see in a few minutes. Just think water." Arnold said laughing.

Garrison looked at him like he was crazy. His mouth was so dry that's all he's thought about since his last little swallow of water about two hours ago. Tye stopped them and pointed to the game trail and they carefully made their way down it as they didn't need a broke leg on a horse or man. When they got to the bottom the horses were getting hard to control as the smell of water was much stronger now. Each man managed to hold their horse but they were as anxious as the horses. When they rounded a outcropping of rock they saw the pool in the shade of a cliff. It was a small pool and it wasn't the best tasting but it was wet and cool. The men filled their canteens and the small barrel on the pack horse before they let the horses in to drink. They pulled them back after a few seconds and walked them around for a minute before they let them drink their fill. Too much water too fast could kill a horse just as sure as dying of thirst.

Dusk was coming quickly and being where they were, in between two fairly large mountains it would get darker quicker.

"We might as well make camp for the night but not here by the water. Let's move farther back in this canyon, away from it. They moved a quarter of a mile back in the canyon, and it was pitch dark by the time they picketed their horses, fed them some oats and laid out their bedrolls.

"We'll have a cold camp tonight," Tye said. Keep the noise down as sound will travel a long ways in these rocky canyons. We'll have the same watch schedule as last night." He took some jerky, a biscuit, canteen, and his rifle and moved off a ways to start his watch. The night was the same as the previous nights had been. The only sound was an occasional coyote's melancholy howling, the sound of flapping wings of a owl looking for something to eat, and the unpleasant sound of one of the men snoring. The night passed peacefully with each man taking his watch with Tye again taking the first and last.

With dawn coming on they made a fire and boiled coffee and fried bacon.

"We'll stop at the spring on the way out and replace the water we've used and let the horses drink their fill. Tye instructed. "I think we are real close to finishing this patrol...one way or another."

They made their way to the seep and replaced the water they used, then made their way back up the slope to the trail they were on the previous evening. The sun was over the tops of the cliffs now and the temperature was rising. The men immediately broke out in sweat. He thought of Rebecca and wondered if she would be anxious to hug him now the way he knew he smelled. He smiled at the thought of her wrinkling up her pretty little nose and backing off. He would be glad when this thing was over and he could see her again. A little voice in his head reminded him. 'You had better get her out of your mind you idiot and back on the situation here or you might night live to see her again.'

The glint of something on the side of the hill caught Tye's attention and he immediately jerked his horse to the side and an instant later a bullet whispered by where he had been, and then all hell broke loose as bullets were hitting everywhere. He heard the sickening thud of one hitting flesh and turned to see Garrison rolling off his horse. Arnold and Phipps were quicker and were already scrambling behind some boulders. One of their horses was down and thrashing about before Phipps mercifully shot it. Garrison was moaning but there was no way to get to him without exposing himself to the murderous fire.

"Garrison," Tye hollered. "Garrison can you hear me?"

A soft, almost inaudible" yes," came from him followed by some moans.

"Where are you hit?

"Damn shoulder."

"Listen to me," Tye said. "Don't move. If they think you are still alive they will shoot again. Do you understand.?"

"Yeah." came the reply in a whispered voice.

"We'll get you in a few minutes. Arnold, you or Phipps see where those shots came from?"

"No, when you jerked your horse the way you did we were hitting the ground. The Lieutenant was a little slow I guess."

"I saw where the reflection came from but I don't know if they are all in one spot or not."

"Your seeing it when you did sure saved our hides," Phipps said. "What do you want us to do?"

"Sit tight for a minute while I sort things out."

The first thing was to get to Garrison and get him some aid. He thought for a minute about how to best do it without getting his tail shot off. He shut his eyes to think of a plan.

"Well, here we go again. Twice in a week," he thought to himself remembering the ambush at the pay wagon. They had to know where the shooters were. If they didn't fire they couldn't locate them. Simple enough to do that. Give them something to shoot at.

"Listen you two cause I ain't going to do this but once. I'm going to draw their fire and you had better see where they are. On the count of three. ONE, TWO, THREE and he raised up firing blindly and immediately ducked back down as several bullets whizzed by, some striking the boulder he was behind.

"You okay Tye? Arnold hollered.

"Yeah, just bleeding from some damn rock fragments." Tye had cuts on his neck and top of his right hand.

"Did you see where the shots came from?"

"They all came from one spot. I counted four separate smokes and so did Phipps.

"Good, that should mean they are all here. In a minute I want you two to open fire where you saw the smoke. Don't stop till I get Garrison out of the line of fire. Just open up when you are ready."

In a second they were both firing as fast as they could with rifle and pistols. Tye sprinted out and grabbed Garrison by the collar and was dragging him back to where he had been when the Mexicans opened up. They couldn't get a good aim though as Phipps and Arnolds bullets were splattering rocks everywhere. Tye fell back in the hole behind the boulder with Garrison. He was sucking air from the exertion and partially from the excitement of what he just did.

"Way to go, Tye," Arnold hollered. " Is he okay.?"

"He'll live but he's going to be down for awhile," Tye answered.

"You two reload and give me a minute to catch my breath, and we'll do the next step in ending this thing."

"We're already reloaded, Tye, just give the word," Phipps hollered.

Tye, laying on his back, had caught his breath and said a little prayer, then hollered.

"Give me some covering fire and I'm going to injun around behind them and get them in a cross fire."

"We're ready anytime you are."

'NOW", Tye said and scooted back down the hill as the two started firing. He reached the bottom and started working his way carefully and quietly around to the right, down a draw that kept him completely out of sight from the Mexicans on the hill above him. When he figured he had gone far enough to the right he started up the hill. He immediately dropped back down as he heard rocks rattling from above.

'The sonofabitches are trying to flank us too.' Tye thought to himself. He quietly scooted behind a boulder and waited. It was quiet as the firing had stopped from above them. He was sweating profusely and his heart was beating rapidly with the excitement. He heard the rocks again and knew the Mexican was close, damn close. He wished he could melt into the rock wall and disappear for a minute. All of a sudden the Mexican jumped into the draw right in front of him, his back to Tye. A true fighting man has a sense that tells him when danger is close. He must have felt Tye was there as he immediately turned to face him, a look of surprise on his face. He was bringing his rifle up when Tye brought his rifle down like a club, striking and breaking the man's wrist. The Mexican dropped his rifle as pain shot up his arm. Tye dropped his rifle and whipped out his Bowie and before the man could holler a warning buried it to the hilt in the man's stomach, just below the breast bone. A look of shock was on the man's face as Tye clamped his left hand over the mans mouth to squelch a scream. Blood was coming from his mouth and oozed between Tye's fingers. He struggled for a few seconds and then his eyes set as Tye slowly let him fall to the ground. Tye wiped his hand in the sand and his knife on the man's pants. He picked up his rifle and checked the barrel to make sure it had not gotten clogged with sand. He blew the sand out of the firing mechanism and the shell chamber and then wiped it clean with the dead mans shirt.

Tye started up the hill, crawling from rock to rock and cactus to cactus, trying to stay out of sight and be quiet at the same time. He was angling to the right as he climbed making sure he would flank them. There was only sporadic fire coming from both positions now. From the sound of the shots from the Mexicans, he knew he was coming up behind them.

"Only a little bit further and you'll have them," he thought to himself. He kept climbing.

"There he is below and beyond them," Arnold said to Phipps.

"Yeah, I see him. Make sure you're loaded and ready when he opens up."

Tye was in position high enough and was now crawling to his left trying to locate the men. When he finally saw them, he was about fifty yards behind and above them.

He checked his rifle again to make sure it wasn't clogged with dirt from all the climbing. He zeroed in and for the first time in his life was going to shoot a man in the back. He started squeezing the trigger but stopped and released the pressure. He just could not do it, not in the back.

"Alex, you want to surrender," he shouted.

Startled, it took a second for them to react and then they were swinging their rifles to bear on him. Tye fired before they were ready and the man on the extreme left jerked and fell down the slope, rolling over and over before stopping in a patch of cactus. He ducked as the shots came his way. He looked around the boulder he was behind and saw another man rolling down the hill that either Arnold or Phipps shot. That left only one man. From his build, he figured it was Alex. He could see him looking at where Arnold and Phipps were, then at where Tye was. He knew he was a dead man at that point if he tried to fire his rifle. He threw his rifle and pistol out and stood up with his hands held high. Tye stood up and motioned the Mexican to move down the hill. He kept his rifle on him all the way down to where his men were. They threw him on the ground and bound his hands behind his back and then roughly jerked him to his feet. Tye walked, slid and fell down the steep slope to where they were. He turned the Mexican around to look at him. He was sure it was Alex because of his build and the scar.

"You Alex Vasquez?" Tye asked.

The man spit at him. Tye backhanded him across the mouth with his hand knocking him down and Arnold roughly jerking him back up.

"One more time, are you Alex Vasquez?"

The man stared at Tye saying nothing. Tye doubled up his fist and buried it about six inches in the man's stomach. All the air was gone from him and he was doubled over, gasping for some of the precious stuff to fill his lungs.

"One more time. Are you Alex Vasquez?"

The man nodded his head.

"Del go get the money off the two that rolled down the hill." As Del walked off, Tye hollered at him, "Make damn sure they are dead before you start going thru their pockets.

"One here, and two up there. Where's the fourth man?" Phipps asked.

"Oh yeah, the fourth one is down in that draw. I met him as he was trying to flank us. He didn't make it." Phipps looked at Tye and shook his head.

Tye sat down, totally drained of all energy. He took a long drink of water and stared at Alex.

"I've never seen a hanging before, Alex. I hear they are not pretty to watch but I think I will enjoy watching yours.

"We ain't back to Texas yet, gringo. I've got friends over here and my brother, Frank, is in Texas. You got no one, gringo."

"So you speak English. That's good," Tye said. I don't know about your friends over here but your brother, Frank, he ain't going to be helping you none. He met up with Tanza and met a long, terrible death."

Tye could see some of the pompousness go out of him. Tye walked over and took a fat wad of bills from him just as Arnold and Phipps returned with the money from the other three. The three had a total of nineteen hundred and sixty dollars between them. Alex had over eight thousand in his pockets and saddle bag.

" That sonofbitch didn't divvy up the money very equal did he." Arnold said laughing.

" Sure looks like he didn't exactly spread it evenly around." Phipps added. "Counted it out four for him and one for everyone else."

Tye figured up the total from all the Mexicans and it was roughly about two thirds, maybe a little more, of the amount stolen. Not bad he thought, but God, what a price. Ten or twelve men dead and three more going to hang.

They bandaged up the Lieutenant as best they could and got him on a horse. They tied Alex legs to the horse so they would not have to worry about him. They started back toward Texas, and home.

When they finally crossed the river, it had been six days since they left Fort Clark. It seemed a lot longer. When they hit the Old Mail Road, Tye sent Phipps ahead to give Thurston a report which Garrison had written. He figured Thurston should know as soon as possible and with Garrison's injury, they were moving slowly. He knew Thurston had probably been a nervous wreck ever since they had left.

When they arrived at the Fort, Thurston was the first to greet them. Tye shook his hand and accepted the thanks and all the pats on the back but he was looking for someone and not paying much attention to anything else. His eyes were desperately searching faces but he could not find her. He began to panic, what if something happened to----he saw her, standing with O'Malley. He started toward her and she was running to him. Seeing her running toward him only confirmed what he already knew, she was the one thing that made living worth while. One more chore to do and she would be his forever

~

Tye heard hangings were something no God fearing Christian man should be enthused about seeing. Tye was thinking they must not be many Christians around here if that was true because it seems everyone in the whole territory was in Brackettville for the hanging Saturday. It had been a week since Tye and his group had brought in Alex Vasquez. Tye was sitting at a table by himself drinking a beer in his favorite saloon listening to all the talk concerning the hanging. He had come in here to have a beer and relax but that was impossible with all the commotion going on. The triple hanging of Alex and his two companions, Jesus and Miguel, was bringing people out of the woodwork. Most of the talk was centering on how Alex was going to meet his maker:.. taking it like a man or whimpering like a baby. Everyone had their opinion and some were getting out of hand which isn't unusual when you mix men and alcohol.

"Bet that big bad Alex will whimper like a baby when the time comes for him to climb those stairs." said a big burly looking gent that from the look of his clothes, was a trapper.

"If you feel that way Senor, put some money where your mouth is." A well dressed Mexican said loudly obviously looking for trouble. He had a pistol that was hung low and he looked like he could use it.

"That man is a pistolero." Tye said to himself. He pulled his pistol and held it under the table. He wasn't going to sit by and watch a murder.

The trapper turned and looked at the Mexican. "Hell, don't get your bowels in a uproar. I didn't mean nothing by it. Just stating my opinion like I always do."

"Then maybe Senor, you should keep your stupid opinions to yourself."

The trapper doubled up his fist and started toward the Mexican when he stopped suddenly. He was looking at the wrong end of a pistol that had appeared out of no where. "Maybe we should take this outside, Senor." The Mexican said.

The trapper looked around for help but saw none in the mostly Mexican crowd. He looked back at the man holding the gun." Hell, man, everyone knows I run my mouth a lot. Come on over here and let me buy you a drink." He turned and yelled at Jim, the bartender. "Jim, bring two more beers over."

The bar had gotten real quiet when the exchange started but now was back in full swing, seeing how there wasn't going to be a fight. Fights was as common out here as breathing. Everyone had their opinions on things and just about everyone had a beer or two every day which only added to the fire. Out here a man was measured by two things, his word and his courage. You had better do what you say and you had better never back down from a fight. It didn't make a damn whether you won or lost the fight, but you had better fight if challenged.

Tye discreetly reholstered his pistol and picked up his beer.

"Well, it's been a hell of two weeks." He thought to himself. "Tracked down the most vicious and cruel bandit in the territory, lost some good friends, and got myself engaged." He had promised to wed Rebecca when he got back off this last patrol but they had discussed the situation concerning the missing Turley children and decided to wait and see if Tye could get them back. The only reason he was here at the Fort now was he had no idea where to look for them. He figured Tanza would come across the border before long and start raising hell and he would be on his trail immediately. He got up to leave to go see the Major to see if any reports had come in when he was stopped by his friend, Jim, the saloon owner.

"Tye, just between you and me, how do you think that sonofabitch is going to handle walking up those steps to the gallows."

Tye rubbed the back of his neck and thought for a minute before speaking. "I watched his brother get scalped alive and never uttered a sound. I figure Alex will walk up those steps and spit in the hangman's face and then tell everyone that's there to go to hell."

"Bout what I thought too. Are you still going after those children, the Turleys."

"Just as soon as I get a line on where the murdering Apache is."

"Only met Mr. Turley once. Never met his wife."

"They were good people, Jim. The best. Sorta like second parents to me after my parents died."

He shook Jim's hand and turned and walked across the road to the bridge over Los Moras Creek that separated Brackettville and Fort Clark. He noticed the sign as he walked over the bridge. It read, *When you cross Los Moras, your sins are washed away.* I hope that's true he thought to himself cause some of these troopers coming back from a night over in Brackettville can use all the help they can get. He laughed at the thought. It was mid-afternoon and with a low cloud cover was unusually cool for a July day in this part of the country. Looking at the clouds Tye thought it was going to storm tonight. "Cool as it is it, may hail too." He mumbled to himself.

He was amazed every time he crossed the bridge. The territory for a hundred miles in every direction was a dry, arid, and inhospitable country but here at Clark, it was like a oasis. For about a square mile, the grass was thick and trees were plentiful. It was absolutely an amazing place. He heard his name called and saw the Major's orderly waving to get his attention. Tye walked toward him.

"Glad I found you Tye. The Major is looking for you and sent me to get you there straightaway."

"You found me so let's go see what the man wants."

~

When Tye walked into headquarters, Thurston saw him and hollered at him to come in to his office. Once in, Thurston told him to shut the door and take a seat. He could tell Thurston was upset. Thurston walked to the wall map and put a finger on a spot southwest of the Fort about thirty or so miles away. It was an area that Tye was intimately familiar with because it was the area where he was raised. In fact, the old homestead place was still there and in good shape since he made it a point every chance he got to spend a couple days there keeping it and his parents graves fixed up.

"Tanza's back. I just received a report of a homestead hit about here."

Tye got up and walked to the map where he could get a closer look. The Major continued. " According to the report, a man and his wife and teenage son were killed. A seven year old was missing.

"Eight years old." Tye said slamming his fist against the wall. That looks like where the Nelsons live. Their youngest is eight years old. " Dammitt, Major. This has got to stop. How quick can you get a patrol in the field.?"

Thurston smiled. "Already done Tye. They will be ready within the hour. Captain McClellan will be leading it."

"McClellan! Tye shouted. Why in the hell is he leading the patrol? You know me and him don't see eye to eye on anything."

Thurston threw up his hands to stop Tye's raving. "Captain Delacruz is in San Antonio. Captain Forsyth is in the hospital sick. Lieutenant Garrison is still recovering from his wound received in the shootout with Alex. Lieutenant Mason is on a three day patrol north of here and Lieutenant Nix is on patrol west of the Fort. The others are all too green for this patrol."

"McClellan." Tye said disgustingly. "Damn."

"Just make the best of it and find Tanza and try and get those children back."

"I'll be ready in thirty minutes." Tye said. "I need to see Rebecca first." He left excited about Tanza being back but he hoped that it wasn't the Nelsons place he hit.

It was going to be dark within the hour. It would be the first time a patrol left at night instead of the daytime or early morning that he had scouted for.

~

Thirty miles to the south, the man standing on his porch lighting his evening smoke was oblivious to the black eyes that were watching his every move. Unknown to him, sure death was fifty yards away in the rocks. The man's two teenage sons came out on the porch to watch the sunset with their father after a hard day's labor.

"Got a lot done today didn't we Pa." Ben, the youngest said.

His pa wasn't listening as he was staring at the rocks at the base of the cliff where Tanza lay with his men.

"What's matter pa, see something?" Jim the oldest asked.

"Get my rifle and bring it to me."

Ben returned with the gun and handed it to his pa as he was trying to figure out what was going on.

"Apaches." Jim whispered and a look of sheer panic crossed the young Bens face as all the color drained from it.

"AIYEEEE!" Came the scream that always had a terrible affect on a white man.

"IN THE HOUSE,QUICK." The father screamed as Tanza and the others rose up and fired their rifles. Bullets riddled all three. The father and Ben were killed instantly and Jim was hit in the leg and lower back. The mother came out and reached down to help Jim as the second volley came. A bullet hit Ben in the back of the head and red gore sprayed into his mother face. Three bullets hit her immediately and she fell forward onto the porch, her hand moving slightly to touch her husbands before she died. A family's hopes, dreams, and future, wiped away in five seconds. Tanza and his band was on them quickly, stripping them of anything useful and then scalping them. They ransacked the house taking food and ammunition. A fire in the middle of the room was lit and quickly spread. They left hollering and screaming, waving the bloody scalps.

Tanza was a Lipan Apache. He had led a small band from the reservation about three months earlier. He had had a lot of success so far, having killed about fifteen settlers and an unknown number of Mexicans in Mexico. With each success, more braves were joining him. His number now was twenty- five seasoned warriors. A formidable force considering the Apaches' fighting ability. He and his men had left the reservation and vowed never to return. The white man had lied, cheated, and stole from them. He would never trust another as long as he lived. A few more victories and more men would flock to him. He needed a victory over the bluecoats or maybe kill the white scout, Watkins. He could become as great a warrior as Cochise in Arizona or maybe even Loco or Juh-hah. His name would be spoken with reverence in the wickiups of his people. He rode away from the burning homestead feeling good, feeling invincible.

~

Tye had said his goodbyes to a tearful Rebecca, stopped at his quarters to get his rifle, buckskin shirt, and other items he would need on the patrol. When he got to the stables, McClellan and the patrol were waiting. His new horse, Sandy, was saddled and waiting for him. Sandy had been a gift from Thurston for his bringing in Alex and recovering so much of the stolen payroll. He was a sorrel like his horse that was shot from under him three weeks earlier. He was big, over seventeen hands high, and looked like he could run. "I hope he has some bottom like my old horse had." he mumbled to himself. His old horse could run forever and had gotten him out of more than one jam.

"If you are ready Mr. Watkins, we can get started." McClellan said sarcastically. Tye never acknowledged him and rode toward and over the bridge over Los Moras and turned west and kicked Sandy into a gallop. He would get out front about a quarter of a mile, then bring him to a walk. Tye couldn't figure out why McClellan had a burr under his butt towards him. He was the only officer in the Fort that he just could not get along with. It worried him more than a little on this trip because he was sure it was going to get bloody and if McClellan refused to listen to anyone, the blood may be mostly theirs.

They were on the Old Mail Road and the traveling was easy for now. About half way to Camp Verde, they would leave the road and head southwest toward the reported attack on the homesteaders. By traveling all night, Tye figured they should arrive shortly after daylight. It was darker than sin right now but by traveling on the road as they were, it would not be a problem. The clouds had moved on and the moon should be up by the time they would turn off the road and head cross country. They were lucky that a full moon would be out to help them see. The land south was rocky and laced with deep arroyos. You were taking a hell of a risk traveling in that terrain if it was pitch dark.. The rocks, bleached white by the sun, would reflect what light the moon provided making it possible to easily see the trail.

It was close to midnight when Tye halted and waited for the patrol to catch up. He crossed his leg over the pommel on the saddle, took out the makings and rolled a smoke. He cupped his hand around the match when lighting the cigarette to keep the flare of the match down. He wasn't worried about Apaches here though- maybe in a couple or three hours when they got into the rougher country. Besides, unless it was unavoidable, Apaches like some of the other tribes, did not like fighting at night. If you were killed at night, they believed you would wander in darkness forever. He was sitting relaxed, stroking Sandy's neck, when he heard the patrol coming long before he could see them.

"This where we turn southwest, Watkins?" McClellan asked.

It grated Tye that the man insisted on calling him by his last name. "Yes sir. You might consider a short break to rest the horses and give them some water." Tye suggested.

"SERGANT!"

Sergeant O'Malley rode up to McClellan. "Yes sir."

"Sergeant, have the men dismount and take care of their mounts. We're taking a fifteen minute break."

Tye was surprised. That was the first time McClellan had done anything he suggested without an argument. He dismounted and loosened the saddle girth on Sandy. He put some water in his hat for him to drink and then gave him some oats to eat. He took some jerky out of his saddle bag, walked over to a large rock and sat down on it.

He noticed all the troopers had taken care of their mounts before themselves. "At least we have some seasoned men on this patrol and not a bunch of pilgrims that have to be led by the hand ever step of the way." he said under his breath. He looked up at the sky. "Probably going to rain in a day or so." He said to O'Malley and McClellan when they walked up.

"What makes you think that?" O'Malley asked, looking up at the cloudless night sky.

"Ring around the moon." Tye said. " Pa always said that was a sign of rain. Found it to be true most of the time."

McClellan looked at the sky, shook his head and walked off. "What does he have against me, O'Malley? Far as I know I ain't ever said or did anything to disrespect him." Tye asked while watching McClellan walk off.

"Don't know for sure, Tye. Got me a idea though." O'Malley answered. "If I had to give an answer, I would say it was that he was jealous of you."

"Jealous!" An astonished Tye said. "What the hell do I have that he would be jealous of?"

"Respect of every man on the Fort. That's something he wants but doesn't have. It's just a guess though."

Tye shook his head in disbelief. "I'll tell you something else Tye." O'Malley continued. "If he gets a chance to discredit you in any way he will. You make a mistake, he'll make damn well sure everyone from Thurston to whomever in San Antonio at district headquarters knows about it."

Tye stood there looking at his friend's old craggily face for a moment, shook his head and walked over to Sandy and started scratching him between the ears. "People are damn funny, ole boy." He said in a soft voice to Sandy. "Never thought anyone would be jealous of me...unless it was because of Rebecca being mine." he added laughing. Sandy snorted and shook his head as if he understood, bringing another smile to Tye. Tye liked this horse. He seemed to understand everything he said. 'Always helps if you have a understanding horse.' Tye thought to himself smiling. He tightened the saddle girth and mounted up and started southwest, away from the Mail Road. He passed McClellan. McClellan jumped up and ordered O'Malley to get the patrol ready to move out immediately. They were moving within a minute with McClellan barely keeping Tye in sight.

It was well after midnight when Tye pulled up suddenly. "Smoke." he said and sat there trying to get a direction the smell was coming from. There wasn't any breeze at all or he would have no problem figuring the direction. He kept sniffing the air and finally figured what direction the faint smell was coming from. He had smelled that smell before and knew it wasn't a campfire. The patrol arrived shortly thereafter. "Watkins, your position is out in front, not with us." McClellan said sarcastically.

"You don't have to tell me where I'm supposed to be McClellan. If you will take a second and take a whiff of the air you will see why I stopped." McClellan started to say something but decided against it and sniffed a couple times. He turned his head and smelled again. "Campfire. There's a campfire close by."

"It's a fire okay but it ain't no campfire." Tye said

"Would you please enlighten us as to what it is then Mr. Watkins?"

"Smelled that smell before. It's a homestead and burned flesh."

"I thought you said we wouldn't be at the homestead before daylight."

"We ain't at the homestead we were going to." Tye said.

"If we are not at the hom..." McClellan stopped in mid sentence. " A different one? Are you saying they have burned another one?"

"I'm guessing that's right. Lets me and you take a look-see."

McClellan turned in his saddle and spoke to O'Malley. "I am going with Watkins to see this homestead that he says is close by. Have the men take a break. We'll be back in a few minutes."

They hadn't gone but a couple hundred yards when they saw the homestead, or what used to be a homestead. The adobe walls were still standing but the roof had fallen inside and small flames could still be seen in places.. "Leave the horses here, Sir. I don't need any more tracks over the ones that are there. Walking to the smoldering remains of the home they saw the burned and blacken bodies stacked together on what was the porch.

"Oh My God!" McClellan said as he saw the remains. "My God."

Tye looked around at the scene. "We can't do anything here till daylight, Sir. Let's go back and make camp and I'll scout the area and get a direction in the morning."

McClellan had never seen anything like that before and he was visibly shook up. "We can wait a minute if you like, Captain." Tye knew most of the men did not like McClellan and it would not help matters if they saw him like this.

"Th...Thanks T...Tye." McClellan stammered out. "I've been on a lot of patrols, but I have never seen anything like that before. Hell, I haven't even had any action yet with bandits or hostiles on any of them." He took a long drink of water from his canteen." Let's go." he said.

"I've seen it more times than I can remember in the last few years and I was like you the first time I saw it. You never get used to it. Captain, this attack was only a few hours ago. I can pick up the Apaches' direction of travel in the morning and if its not in the direction of the other homestead we need to send some men there to take care of the bodies."

"How will they find it?" McClellan asked.

"Send Corporal Davis. He's a good man. Good head on his shoulders and he can read a little sign and follow tracks. I can give him easy directions to the place and then he can double back and cut our trail and catch up."

"Do you think it's a good idea to split the patrol. That will make the Apaches almost equal our number."

"Probably not, Captain, but the dead has to be taken care of and the men should be back with us by dark tonight if I'm right on the direction I think Tanza is going. I'm betting he went south or maybe a little southeast. There are several homesteads in that direction and the bastard has his blood lust up in high gear." Tye took a knee and picking up a stick drew a rough map on the ground showing where they were now and where the other homestead they were looking for was. He then drew a line where he figured the Apaches were headed and it wasn't far to the east of where the other homestead was located. "Davis can head due east after taking care of the dead and cut our trail." He paused to let McClellan think for a minute. He knew it was against army policy to split a force to where you were venerable. He then added. " Course if they ain't headed in the direction I figure, we can do away with that plan."

"We will do it your way." McClellan said. That surprised the hell out of Tye. He then thought about it for a minute and figured the Captain hoped something would happen after he suggested the plan and he would put all the blame on Tye.

Tye knew where a small spring was that was less than a quarter of a mile from where they were. He and the Captain mounted their horses and made their way back to the patrol then headed for the spring to make camp for the night, what there was left of it.

◆ XV ◆

Dawn found Tye making his way back to the camp. He scouted the burned out homestead and the Apaches headed in the direction he figured they would. A burial detail would be selected by McClellan and then they would be on their way.

The land where they were now was broken and had hills and a few arroyos. Where they were headed was going to be much rougher and very condusive to ambush. Tye wasn't too concerned about an ambush yet because he didn't figure Tanza knew anyone was on to them this quick. It would come though. Apaches sometimes appear to be able to talk to the hawks and crows that were always flying over this arid country and told the Apache where their enemies were. Only a couple of times had Tye been able to ambush a band of Apaches, and both times they were young bucks. Tanza was not a young buck but a older, fierce warrior, who was battle tested with not only the bluecoats but the Comanche and the Kiowa. You wouldn't fool him in a hundred years of trying unless you just had blind luck on your side.

After breaking camp, they rode back to the homestead to take care of the bodies. Tye took McClellan and

O'Malley to some rocks at the base of a hill. He showed them where the Apaches had laid in wait.

"They moved in while the people were inside eating the evening meal. When they came out on the porch, probably to have a smoke and look at the sunset, they were shot down." He showed them several shell casings that were on the ground.

"How many were here?" McClellan asked while picking up a casing and smelling of it.

"Only part of the band. Probably no more than six or seven. They tied their ponies about a half mile over younder." Tye said, pointing toward another hill.

"Why in hell's name would they leave their horses way over there and walk that far? With these rocks and hills they could have rode right up to these rocks." the Captain questioned.

"The settlers had some horses in the corral and horses have excellent eyesight. They also can smell when a horse is near that they don't recognize. They would start stomping and snorting and would have alerted the people inside. That's something you need to remember. If you are camped out, the horses are generally your best sentries."

"If what you say is true, then the hostiles have about a eleven or twelve hour head start on us." McClellan stated.

"About right." Tye replied. "If you can have some men take care of these people and send Davis to the other homestead, we can be on our way in a few minutes."

A burial detail was put together with shallow holes being dug in the rocky ground and the charred bodies were placed in them with rocks being placed over them. McClellan spoke a few words over them, then the patrol moved out toward the south following the hostiles. Davis and his detail headed southwest to take care of the other homesteaders.

Before Tye took his normal position out front, McClellan asked him a question. "Why, after two different sets of killing, would Tanza keep going deeper into Texas instead of heading back to the safety of Mexico? He surely would know that we would be after him."

"Tanza doesn't give a tinkers damn about the US Cavalry, Sir. He ain't afraid of us. He has a hate for the white man that's deep and it ain't ever going to change. He wants to kill all the people settling on their land, or what the Apaches consider their land. Truthfully, I honestly think he wants a fight with us. With a victory, Apaches would flock to him like bees to honey. He would be big medicine to them and we can't let that happen. If you ever got a hundred or more Apaches together at one time, this country would see a bloodbath like never before. No one would be safe, not even the cavalry. We have been lucky so far that its always been small groups, ten to twenty-five. One of these days though, you will see them get smart and the Lipan, White Mountain, Mescaleros, Chiricahuas, and all the other tribes of the Apache Nation will get together for a final push to get rid of the hated Pinda-Lickoyee."

"Pinda-Lickoyee?" McClellan said questionably.

"White eyes." Tye said over his shoulder as he rode to take his place in front of the patrol.

As they started out O'Malley moved up beside McClellan and was silent for a moment before speaking. "Sir, I would like to speak to you...off the record."

McClellan looked at him for a second, and then looked straight ahead. "Go ahead Sergeant, speak your mind."

O'Malley spit a wad of tobacco juice at some unknown target on the ground and started speaking. "Captain, I am going to speak my mind and if'n you want me to shut up, just say the word."

McClellan knew that to Major Thurston, O'Malley was second only to Tye in having his respect so he figured he had better listen.

"Go ahead. Speak your mind Sergeant."

"I don't know what it is that you have against Tye, Captain but I will tell you one thing. These men, myself included, owe that man a lot. He has saved our asses more than once from being killed by decisions made by officers like yourself who think they are a little better than anyone else. The men love him and every time you try and belittle him it only puts a bigger rift between you and them. You need them, Sir. You need their respect but you ain't going to get it the way you are going. The other officers have listened to him and taken his advice. They have never gotten men killed unnecessarily like some officers have who knew every damn thing there was to know and if it wasn't in the manual, they wouldn't do it. That's all I got to say," and dropped back to his position behind McClellan. McClellan rode like a man in a trance, not believing what he had just heard. His mind was racing trying to figure out what to do about O'Malley's tirade. It was against army regulations for a non-com to speak to an officer in that manner even if was off the record, so to speak. He turned in the saddle and ordered O'Malley to come back up beside him.

As O'Malley moved in beside him, he figured he was in trouble for what he had said and was surprised when McClellan spoke. "What is this mystique, this almost God like worship about Tye, Sergeant. Why does everyone think he is so damn great?"

"Ain't no mystique, Captain. I've been in this man's army since '57. Been out here on the frontier since after the War. I've seen fifty scouts come and go. Not a one of them could carry Tye's moccasins. Tye knows the Apache better than the damn Apache knows himself. He can track as good as, or better'n most Apaches. He is an expert at hand-to-hand combat whether with fist, knives, or tomahawk. He knows the land. Hell, he hadn't never lived more fifty miles from where he was born, which by the way isn't far from here. No patrol he's ever been on as been ambushed. That's enough reason to love him right there. He's risked his own neck more than once to save a man. I know, for a fact Captain that you have never been in a fight with the Apache. When it happens, and you hear those shrieks and screams from the throats of the Apaches, and the bullets are flying in every direction, and every where you look, men are dying, you see Tye, calm as if he was on his porch back at the Fort and you get the feeling that you will make it because he is there. He, Captain, is a special breed, just as his pappy was. When things get tight, you had better listen to him or you may not have a future. That's no reflection on you Sir. I would tell Major Thurston the same...but he already knows it."

"Thank you for your candor, Sergeant. That's all." McClellan said as O'Malley once again dropped in behind him. It was late afternoon now and McClellan was hoping the patrol led by Corporal Davis would show up. He figured they should have caught up by now.

"Tye's coming." a voice from behind him said.

"Damn." McClellan said to himself when he realized he had been in another world mentally and did not see Tye coming. "It could have been a damn Apache and I would not have seen him. You had better get your head out and your mind on business and quick."

"Ole Tanza is taking his time. We've made up about three or four hours." Tye said as he rode up to McClellan.

"Good, let's get going and make up some more time." McClellan said excited that they were getting closer.

"Hold on, Captain." Tye said. "It won't do you or us any good to catch them and the men and horses be used up so bad neither can function as they are supposed to. We have been pushing the men and horses for almost twenty-four hours straight. They are bushed. My suggestion would be to make a camp before dark so they can have a fire for a hot meal and get some rest as well as the horses. We can get going again about two hours before daylight. That will still be a couple hours before Tanza heads out. Like I said, he ain't hurrying none."

McClellan thought for a moment, remembering what O'Malley told him. "Sergeant, have the men make camp. No fires after dark. Set the roster for sentry duty also."

"Yes sir, Captain." O'Malley said smiling and gave a wink and a nod to Tye.

Every man took his mount and gave him some water and then a rub down before giving him his oats. The men then took care of their personal needs. The meal was hot biscuits and jerky with strong, scalding coffee. The men were in good spirits and the usual joshing and off color jokes were floating around. The fires were put out as darkness settled in around them. Things quieted down as men settled in their bedrolls. Tye, as he usually did, was enjoying the beautiful night sky before the moon came up and took away the brightness of the stars when O'Malley sat down beside him.

"McClellan say anything to you about me yet?"
"No. What are you talking about?" Tye asked.
"We had a discussion a little earlier about you."
"Me. What about me?"
"He asked me why all the men, including Thurston, thinks you hung the damn moon. So I told him why. I also added that if he had any sense he would listen to you."
"You told him that.. If he had any sense." Tye said laughing so hard he had to lay back down.
"Aye! That is what I told him." O'Malley answered and was laughing too as some of the troopers looked on and wondered what was happening that was so funny that would have the usually stoic First Sergeant laughing like that. They both got control of themselves when they saw some of the men looking at them.
"I'm sure he will have something to say before long." Tye said, trying to keep a straight face. "Lets get some sleep."

~

As always when on patrol, the men were mustered out of their bedrolls a couple hours before dawn. This morning, it was even earlier and the mood was more urgent. The men knew they had made up a lot of time yesterday with their extended march. Maybe with another one today they would catch up to the hostiles tomorrow and get this thing over with. A quick breakfast and they were on their way well before daylight. Tye decided to stay with the patrol till after sunrise instead of out front. He wasn't worried about Tanza right now.

By mid morning Tye was a quarter of a mile out front when he smelled wood smoke. He quickly dismounted and made his way on foot toward the smell. He found the source, the abandoned camp of the Apaches. They hadn't been gone more than two, maybe three hours by the look of the horse droppings and smoldering coals of their campfires. He back tracked to his horse and was mounting when the patrol arrived. "Camp is about a hundred yards further up the canyon, Captain. They've been gone maybe three hours."

"We're three hours behind them!" An astonished McClellan said.

"Yeah, and that bothers me some." Tye said looking up the trail where the Apaches had gone.

"What do you mean?"

"Apaches can cover fifty or sixty miles a day, Captain. More than that if they are pushed. This bunch covered about twenty miles yesterday. It's almost like they know we are here and are letting us close in."

"That information makes this old Irishman feel real damn comfortable Tye." O'Malley said chuckling.

"Well you may be comfortable but I'm damn uncomfortable about things." Tye said in a serious tone. "Captain, may I suggest you make sure you keep me in sight and tell your men no stinking dozing in the saddle. Tell them to keep their rifles out and handy."

"Pass the word, Sergeant." McClellan said.

~

It was midafternoon and it was hotter than hell in this rocky canyon that Tye was making his way through. He was moving very slowly now, his eyes taking in every detail, searching every place someone could hide... his ears alert for any unnatural sound. He stopped, and using his kerchief, wiped his face and neck, never taking his eyes off the terrain. He dismounted and poured some water into his hat and gave Sandy a drink. He took a swallow and remounted and started again. This was nerve racking work but Tye loved it. Made you feel alive he would say. The canyon walls were almost sixty feet high at this point. The floor of the canyon was littered with huge boulders, some half as big as a fair sized house. He was looking at tracks when Sandy's ears twitched. Tye looked up and saw sunlight reflect off something. He immediately threw himself from Sandy just as a bullet broke the air where he had been. He hit the ground hard and scrambled back to Sandy and pulled his rifle out of the saddle scabbard just as another bullet hit the pommel causing Sandy to bolt. Tye jumped behind a large boulder and checked his rifle to make sure it was cocked. He was going to try and injun up on the shooter, or shooters, and nothing was worse than having an enemy in sight and him hearing the distinct metallic sound of a rifle being cocked. He took off his hat and looked over the rock to where he thought the shooter was.

~

McClellan jerked his head sharply when he heard the first shot. "O'Malley, what do you make of it."

"They ain't shooting at us, Sir. Tye found himself some Apaches."

"You take two men and check it out. Be careful."

"Yes sir. PHIPPS, ARNOLD, FRONT AND CENTER." O'Malley shouted. They were there in less than ten seconds. "Come with me to check out the shooting." They moved out as McClellan watched anxiously. As the three entered the narrow canyon, O'Malley said. " Phipps watch the right, Arnold the left, and don't get trigger happy. Tye is out there."

◆ XVI ◆

Tye decided to make a break for the next boulder, which was about twenty yards away. He took a quick look and broke for the boulder, running in a zig zag pattern. No shots were fired. Tye looked again where the shots had come from. Another thirty yards and he will be directly below him, or them. He took a deep breath and took off again. Once again no shots came his way. 'What the hell!' He thought to himself. 'They should hav..'. He heard a horse whinny farther up the canyon and then heard an Apache shouting, probably Apache cuss words. He knew why no shots were fired. You show a horse as fine as Sandy was and the Apache would drop everything he was doing for a chance to capture him. "Dammit! Sandy." Tye yelled and took off down the bottom of the canyon. He went around a large boulder and ran right into an Apache that was holding Sandy's reins. The Apache was knocked off his feet and under Sandy. Sandy reared and came down with both hooves, one striking the startled Apache in the chest, breaking his sternum and some ribs and the other hoof smashing into his face, crushing it like a egg shell. Tye was getting up off the ground when a blood curdling yell came from behind him. With reflexes honed with years of fighting, Tye threw himself to the side just as the tomahawk came down where his head had been an instant earlier. He drew his knife and turned to face the Apache warrior who had thrown his tomahawk aside and had his Bowie out, facing Tye. He was big for an Apache, probably five foot ten or so- broad thru the shoulders and looked strong as a bear. He had the Apache face, round with a broad flat nose and had streaks of white paint across it and a dirty, red bandana around his head. He was probably twenty-five or so. Tye knew this wasn't going to be easy and probably both would get cut, with one of them dying. He could pull his pistol and shoot him but his sense of fairness wouldn't let him just as he would never shoot a man in the back. The Apache probably could have shot him. They crouched and circled each other warily, each waiting for the other to make the first move.

Tye was sweating profusely from the extreme heat in the canyon and from the strain of the last five minutes. The sweat was stinging his eyes and slightly blurring his vision. The Apache saw this and made his move. He came in low, the knife in his right hand which was almost touching the ground. He come up with the knife trying to catch Tye in the groin. Tye was ready and pared the knife from the Apache easily and caught him on the chin with a left hook that the Apache never saw coming. The Apache was stunned for a couple of seconds but recovered and retaliated in a vicious attack that had Tye backpedaling. The brave got a little over zealous in his attack and made a costly mistake. He missed with one wild swing with the knife and left his midsection open. Tye did not let the mistake get by him as he drove his knife deep in the man's midsection and at the same time hit him with another blow to the chin with his left. This time the brave's knees buckled and he fell forward, flat on his face. His body jerked a couple pf times then was still. Tye leaned against a boulder trying to catch his breath. Tye checked the other one and saw he was dead. He stood up and walked to where an excited Sandy, eyes bulging, was stomping and snorting. Tye's voice calmed him enough to where he could get hold of the reins to control him and begin scratching him between the ears. "Thanks old boy. You saved my bacon today."

Tye walked over to the Apache to make sure he was dead when the sound of horses hooves striking rocks startled him and he spun around abruptly, pistol cocked.

"Dammit, O'Malley! You trying to get your ass shot. Damn, man, you don't go riding hell bent for leather up behind a man that's just been in a fight."

"Sorry about that, Tye. We were in a hurry to get here to help." O'Malley said while looking around. "Looks like we were too late." He picked up Tyes hat and handed it to him. "You okay?"

"Yeah. Just a couple scratches is all. Sorry I jumped you a second ago but you've been in enough fights to know better." Tye answered while putting his hat on. "Men have been killed accidentally that way."

"What happened?" O'Malley asked.

"I was looking at the ground for tracks, when I saw Sandy twitching his ears. I looked up and saw the glint of metal on the side of the canyon and threw myself off Sandy just the Apache fired. I heard the bullet as it went by. They tried stealing Sandy and he took care of that one over there with the smashed face and I took care of the other."

They all turned as McClellan and the patrol arrived." Everything okay?" McClellan asked, looking at O'Malley.

"Yes sir. Two hostiles jumped Tye. Both are dead Sir."

"You okay, Mr. Watkins? The Captain asked.

"Yes sir." Tye said while mounting Sandy. " We know that Tanza knows we are back here following him. From now on it will be interesting." He checked his rifle to see if any dirt was clogging the barrel after he dropped it during the fight. He had seen a young Ranger a few years ago have half his face blown off when he fired a rifle with a clogged barrel. It made a lasting impression on him. He put the rifle in the saddle scabbard, turned Sandy, and was gone.

"Sergeant." McClellan said brusquely. "What did Watkins mean by it was going to get interesting?"

"Well, Sir. The Apaches obviously know we are trailing them and they are not running. It's almost like Tye said before... they are taking us somewhere."

"What do you mean by that?"

"Tanza needs a victory over the army to gain that invincible image so that the other young bucks will join him. He has a idea of when and where he intends to do this. Tye is trying to keep us out of trouble long enough for him to figure out where and when it's going to happen. That's what Tye meant. He also meant for us to stay sharp, alert, and ready for anything."

It was mid afternoon when Tye stopped and let the patrol catch up to him. "Anything wrong, Watkins?" McClellan asked.

"No, Sir. Just thought maybe the men and horses needed a break. We've been pushing pretty hard in this heat."

"How far behind the hostiles are we now?"

"Maybe two hours."

"Then I think we should press on then." McClellan said.

Tye, leaning forward with both hands on the pommel of his saddle said in a low voice. "Out here, Captain, you need three things to survive. One is water; two is a horse that's not wore down; the third is a weapon that works. The horses are tired and need a break with some water and oats. The men are riding with their chins on their chest. I have not seen you nor any of the men clean and inspect their weapons since we left the Fort. A break is just a suggestion, Captain. You do what you think is best."

McClellan glared at Tye for a moment and almost signaled for the patrol to move out but decided not to and told O'Malley to tell the men they were taking a thirty minute or so break. "Sergeant, make sure the men give water and oats to their mounts." Then added. " Tell the men while they are resting that I want them to clean their weapon and make sure they are in good working order."

"Yes sir." O'Malley said, miffed that the Captain thought he had to tell the men to take care of their mounts.These were not raw recruits but men who had been thru this before. Tye was surprised when he saw the Captain and the men cleaning their weapons. It brought a smile to his face. "Maybe there is hope for that man yet." he mumbled under his breath.

McClellan was thru taking care of his weapons and was sitting on a rock thinking about Tye and what O'Malley had said. McClellan wanted to make a career out of the army and he didn't want any blemishes on it, especially one getting men killed following his orders that were bad decisions on his part. Maybe O'Malley's right. I should listen to Tye and what his suggestions are. At least, if anything happens I could lay it on him. He smiled at that.

It was late afternoon and Tye was out front, checking tracks. He was almost a half mile out in front now and he had all his senses working overtime. All the signs pointed to trouble coming and pretty quickly. From the looks of the tracks, they were no more than a hour or so behind. He looked all around and then mounted Sandy and started forward when shots from behind him caused him to jerk Sandy around and immediately was galloping back to the patrol. He had gone maybe a quarter of a mile when he saw a trooper coming toward him at a dead run.

~

Tanza was livid. He had a trap set for Tye and one for the patrol. The old problem showed itself that haunted all the Indians throughout the history of fighting the army... the problem of individualism. They had their leaders but warriors often made their own decisions at the wrong times, like now. Tanza's plan was for him to shoot Watkins before the trap was sprung on the patrol. He figured with him gone, the rest of the bluecoats would be easy to fool and trap. Some of his braves ruined that by not waiting on him to fire first and kill Watkins. He was squeezing the trigger when the shots were fired. He saw Tye turn and head back toward the patrol and he knew his plan was not going to work. He took the men who were with him and headed toward the canyon where the ambush was set. He needed to get his men out before they were trapped by Tye.

~

"WHAT HAPPENED, TROOPER?" Tye shouted as they met.

"A... Apaches. The Captain chased them. O... O'Malley, h..he was shouting for him to stay but he went anyway." The excited trooper was saying.

"Settle down Corporal. Tell me exactly what happened." Tye already knew that McClellan had fell for the oldest trick of all.

"Three Apaches suddenly appeared to our left and took a couple of shots at us. They didn't hit anything. The shithea..Sorry, Sir.

I mean the Captain took half the patrol and chased them with O'Malley screaming for him not to." They both looked to the southeast as a volley of shots sounded.

"Dammit. They're in the damn ambush now." Tye said. "Corporal, go back to the patrol and have them follow you toward where the shots are coming from. Do not do anything till I tell you to. I will meet you over there." Pointing with his rifle toward a cliff about a mile away.

"Yes sir. Do you think we are too late Sir." The corporal said just as more shots were heard.

"Not as long as shots are being exchanged. Now get going." Tye was beside himself. McClellan should have known better than to fall for that trick. He kicked Sandy and raced toward the sound of the gunfire. When he reached the base of a hill that he figured separated him from the ambush, he dismounted and climbed to the top, carefully looking over the other side thru some sage that kept him from being visible to those he saw below him. He immediately saw what was happening and knew he had better do something quickly. The patrol was pinned down by at least a half dozen Apaches that were on each side of the narrow canyon. He couldn't see, but he knew they would be some at the far end of the canyon to keep the men from escaping that way. He saw two troopers down and apparently dead. One horse was down and he saw two other men that were wounded. He knew from experience that before long, several Apaches would be working their way up the canyon from the other end closing the trap. He scrambled back down the hill, mounted Sandy, and with Tye laying low in the saddle, headed toward the cliff at full speed where he hoped the other men waited.

~

"Should have listened to you Sergeant. I feel like a idiot falling for that trick." McClellan said to O'Malley as they huddled side by side in the cluster of rocks on the canyon floor. They were in a good spot as far as them not being in danger of getting shot by the Apaches on the sides of the canyon but O'Malley knew what was coming. "They will rush us from four sides Captain. Have your pistol and saber out. It will get nasty quick and it will be close in fighting. Don't' think when they come, just shoot and swing that damn saber."

"Do.., do we have a chance?" A nervous McClellan asked.

O'Malley spit some tobacco juice before answering. "Onliest chance we got is Tye. Maybe he can get here before they close in and rush us."

This was McClellan's first encounter with the Apaches, and he was sure it was going to be his last. He accepted the fact he was going to die. Surprisingly, instead of shaking and feeling like he needed to throw up, he was the opposite; relaxed and had a feeling of serenity almost as if he was looking forward to dying. His mind drifted back a few years, before he joined the army...back to the small farm in Georgia he lived on with his parents and two younger sisters. As far back as he could remember he wanted to be a general in the army. He sure didn't want to farm. The toiling under the sun had taken its toll on his father and he died at the age of thirty- nine. They sold the farm and moved to Richmond where his mother was from and still had relatives there. He finished school there and at seventeen, joined the army so he could become a general like he had dreamed of. He was with Sherman on his march through the South. He displayed courage and leadership that was noticed and reported to Sherman. One promotion after another followed and he knew he was on his way to his dream. He was a colonel when the War ended but like many other officers that received field commissions, busted back in rank. He had been a Captain for two years now and after this stupid decision on his part today, probably would be a lieutenant or less by tomorrow...if he was still alive.

~

The rest of the patrol was waiting for him when Tye arrived. He spotted the corporal that had told him what happened. He told the corporal in front of everyone that he was in charge of the patrol.

"When I open up from the top of that ridge, I want you to form a skirmish line and charge down that canyon. Keep your rifles in their scabbards. It will be close in fighting so use your pistols." Tye drew a rough map in the dirt showing where the patrol was pinned down and where the Apaches were so everyone would know what to do. "Be careful. The men are scattered along the floor so make sure it's Apache's you are shooting at. He turned and headed back to the ridge. It had been no more than ten minutes since he was here but when he looked over he saw the trap was almost closed. He took aim at the nearest Apache that was below him. He waited a minute, giving the patrol a little more time to get ready. He got a glimpse of McClellan and O'Malley behind a cluster of large boulders. The Apaches sneaking up the canyon floor were only thirty yards away when Tye whistled and shot the Apache as he turned around. His buddy that was next to him fired at Tye but Tye had rolled to the side and fired his pistol striking the Apache in the chest and knocking him over the rock he had been behind. The Apache rolled head over heels down the steep slope. Tye heard the bugler sounding charge and the hammering of the steel shoes of their mounts echoing off the canyon walls. Apaches were scrambling in front of them to get out of the way and some were cut down by the trooper's pistols and the others were racing up the far canyon walls to get to the safety of the other side. It was over in less than a minute. Tye saw O'Malley wave at him and he acknowledged it with a wave. He made his way down the slope, stopping to check the Apache he had shot first, to make sure he was dead. Reaching the canyon floor he was greeted by several grateful troopers and an obviously embarrassed McClellan. The others arrived from the charge up the canyon in a cloud of dust. "Everyone make it, Corporal?" Tye asked.

"Yes sir." a smiling Corporal shouted." We kilt three of the red bastards coming in."

Tye reached up and patted him on the thigh. "You did good, Corporal. Real Good." The young Corporal grew about a foot in height as he swelled with pride at the praise Tye gave him in front of the men. Tye turned to O'Malley. "How many did you lose?"

"Two dead and a couple nicked. It was fixing to get a lot worse if you hadn't showed up when you did."

"You okay, Captain?" Tye asked.

"I'm fine except for my pride." He mumbled in a low tone.

"Let's get the wounded tended to and the dead wrapped in blankets and get the hell out of this canyon, Captain." Tye suggested.

McClellan, staring at the ground looked up and told O'Malley to take care of it. Tye saw that McClellan had lost his pompousness. He had seen other officers that made a mistake that got men killed and never recovered from it. The guilt, or shame, had broken them and they never made a field officer, most ending up working at desk jobs shuffling papers. He wasn't going to let that happen to McClellan regardless of his personal feelings towards him. He thought McClellan had the backbone to make a good officer if he could smooth out the rough spots.

He walked over to McClellan. "Well, that's out of the way."

McClellan looked up. "What's out of the way?" He asked and was surprised to see Tye smiling.

"Your getting snookered by the Apaches with that trick." Tye answered.

McClellan looked at him questionably. "Captain, there's been damn few officers out here that have not fallen for that trick. You ain't the first and sure as hell won't be the last. Important thing is to learn from your mistakes out here and don't repeat them."

"But two men died from my stupidity!" McClellan said.

"That's part of being a field commander, Captain. Men die in war. It's normal to be remorseful, but you go on and do your job. Everyone makes mistakes. You learn from them and go on. I had plenty of men die in my command when I was leading them with the Rangers. I know it's hard to accept, but you learn to. Now what you need to do is stand straight, look the men in the eyes and continue doing your job. You will, in time, earn their respect. Respect is not something you earn overnight. Respect comes with making good, sound decisions time after time. Do that, Captain, and the men will follow you to hell and back. I think you have the sand to make a fine officer."

McClellan stood there for a few seconds, not knowing what to say. He was shocked at the advice Tye had given him and especially shocked at the confidence Tye apparently has in his ability to lead men after the way he had treated Tye. " Tha..thanks Tye." he finally stammered out. "You're right, I won't make that mistake again." he said smiling. He shook Tye's hand and thought to himself that from now on he was going to be like the others, looking to Tye for advice.

"It's getting late, Captain. Let's find a place to camp for the night." Tye said.

◆ XVII ◆

Back at the Fort, Thurston was pacing the floor. He was a proud man and he was proud of his command at Fort Clark. He wanted to do his job which was to protect the homesteaders from the bandit gangs and the roving bands of Apaches and occasionally, the Comanche. He knew that the settlers were watching, wondering if he could bring down Tanza. They had been happy with him over Alex Vasquez being caught. He was worried about this patrol because of McClellan. He cursed his luck that at the time he had to send them out, he had no other officers available. It wasn't that he was worried that McClellan wasn't a capable officer but he was concerned about his relationship with Tye. McClellan was headstrong and could be hard to get along with at times. He had talked in length about Tye to him, telling him to listen to him and consider his suggestions and advice. He didn't know if McClellan listened to him or not and that bothered him. He told himself that he had better listen to Tye and not do anything stupid to jeopardize this patrol.

Thurston intended to add his name to the list of commanders out here that was helping to make this country a safe place for a man to raise his family. He had sacrificed a lot to get to this position, including his marriage. Nothing or no one was going to keep him from attaining his goals. He had this Fort in good shape. There were five stone buildings that served as the enlisted men's quarters. There was three two-story buildings that had two officers each and their families, if they were married, and the post commander's home. There was a mess hall, hospital, and stables. All were built from rock except the mess hall and were here to stay. Thurston walked to his window and in the evening shadows stood looking proudly at his domain.

~

It was full dark when the patrol settled in for the evening camp. Tye was taking care of Sandy as was the other troopers with their mounts. He gave him a good combing with the brush which he knew Sandy liked. He had given him a healthy drink and extra oats before brushing. Sandy nickered and nipped at Tye's hand. Tye was as fond of this horse as Sandy was of him. A voice suddenly coming from behind him startled him for an instant.

"Tye, that arrogant sonofabitch is going to get us all killed." Corporal Phelps said in a low voice.

Tye turned and answered him in a no nonsense tone. "You men don't worry none about the Captain, Phelps. He's gonna be okay. Just give him a little time. Let me ask you something. Have you ever been on a patrol with a young officer that didn't make any mistakes?"

Phelps thought for a moment. "Only Garrison I guess, and that was because he was so green he didn't take a leak without asking you first if it was okay." he said laughing.

"What do you think of Captain Delacruz?"

Phelps thought for a moment. "He's a find officer."

"You'd follow him anywhere...right?"

"I guess so. Why are you asking about him?"

"Less than two years ago, he fell for the same trap McClellan did and had four men killed. Since then he hasn't made a mistake and you men like him. Is that not right?" Tye asked.

"Yeah, I guess so."

"I rest my case." Tye said smiling. "Tell the men I said give him a chance. He'll do fine."

Tye, finished with Sandy, walked over to his bedroll and sat down beside McClellan. "We've butted heads a few times, Tye," McClellan said, "and I'm sorry for that. I had a long talk with O'Malley a while back and he opened my eyes to some things. I know the army regulations like the back of my hand but like O'Malley told me, that information can get a man killed out here. He said a lot. He spoke to me like I was a stepchild. It would take me two days to write him up." He said laughing. He took a drink of coffee, then continued. "He also told me I was a fool for not listening to you. After the last couple of days, I guess he was right. I can see why Thurston thinks so highly of him...and you. Maybe we can work together a little better." He offered his hand to Tye, which Tye took gladly.

"I knew you had a burr under your saddle for me and I probably didn't help matters with my attitude." Tye replied while shaking his hand.

"I think I'll make my rounds before turning in. See you in the morning." McClellan said. Tye lay back down and looked at the stars. He lay there wondering what all O'Malley had said and listening to a trooper with a pleasant voice singing a old cavalry song known as Fiddlers Green.

"Halfway down the road to hell, in a shady meadow green, are all the souls of dead troopers camped and this eternal resting place is know as Fiddlers Green. So when a man and his charge go down beneath a saber clean and the hostiles come to take your scalp, just empty your canteen, put your pistol to your head and go to Fiddlers Green."

~

Less than five miles away, Tanza was sitting on the side of a hill looking westward, to where his beloved mountains lay in Mexico and remembering how it used to be. It seemed so long ago but in reality, it had been less than two years. He was remembering his family, his father and mother, his grandfather, and his little brother, Two Bears. How happy they were then, hunting and raiding the Mexicans and the Comanche. The feeling of being free to come and go as they pleased. Then the white man came, slow at first, then like a flood, taking the land for their own and killing the game for sport. They wanted the Apache out of the land; out of the land the Apache had been on for generations.

The Apache's fought back but they were always outnumbered and never had enough guns and ammunition. The old ones finally had enough and agreed to go to reservations. On the reservations, things were terrible. Nothing was as promised by the 'White Father' from a place called Washington. The blankets, flour, corn, beans, and cattle were never in numbers as promised on the piece of paper the old ones signed. Tanza had had enough of this, begging like old women for handouts from the white man. He left the reservation with a dozen other young men vowing to never return. They would live like their fathers had lived, free and if need be, die as an Apache warrior should die, in battle. He had some successes and his numbers had grown to almost thirty warriors. Until today, he had not lost a warrior. He had five killed today and three wounded. He intended to make the bluecoats pay and especially, the warrior scout, Watkins. He hated this white man but he respected him as a warrior. Very few white men could ever make an Apache warrior but he figured this one could and probably be a chief. He had a surprise for them in the morning. He smiled at the thought of all the scalps they would have by the time the sun was above the hills.

~

Tye woke up about 1 am and could not go back to sleep. He lay there trying but finally gave up and walked over to where one of the sentries was and rolled a smoke. He knelt down and covered the flare of the match with his hand and lit the smoke.

"Beautiful night ain't it Mr. Watkins." the sentry said.

"Makes a man sorta forget his problems, doesn't it." Tye replied.

"Yes sir, it does. Tell me, Mr. Watkins, do you think we'll catch Tanza this time.?"

Tye looked at him and said. "No, Private, we won't. He will catch us when he wants to."

"What do you mean by that, Sir?"

"Tanza ain't one damn bit afraid of the army, Private. He's not running from us. He's taking us where he wants us. When we get there, he'll let us know." Tye walked over to where the horses were picketed and found Sandy. Sandy dropped his head, expecting to be scratched between the ears. Tye didn't disappoint him. He stood there scratching Sandy and looking toward the east, where Tanza had headed. "He's out there planning, Sandy. I got a feeling we are going to meet him damn quick." He tried putting himself in Tanza's place. " What would I do?" He asked himself. He often did this when tracking someone. More than once he had been right.

A low rumble to the southwest drew his attention. Lightning flashed in the distance and when the sky was lit Tye could see the cloud bank moving in. "We'll be wet by daylight Sandy." It was about 1:30 am when he lay back down. Still, sleep wouldn't come. He lay there for about thirty minutes and finally said to hell with it. He decided he would take a stroll toward the direction Tanza had taken. He told the sentry that he would be back shortly and not to get trigger happy. He walked about a half mile and sat down to take a break and think. He had not even got settled when he heard Apaches talking. He immediately started back to the camp as fast and as quietly as possible. About a hundred yards out he stopped and waited, listening for any sound that was not a normal night sound. He waited about ten minutes when he saw them coming. Twenty- five or so warriors, on foot were approaching the camp. "So this is the spot." he said to himself.

He made his way back to camp, past the sentry and found McClellan. Lightly shaking him, McClellan awoke with a startled look on his face. "Wh..What... Oh, Tye. What's the matter?"

"Tanza. He's here."

"TANZA , HERE N.." He said loudly before Tye could put his hand over his mouth and told him to be quiet.

"Tanza is outside the camp. He will hit us at dawn, probably from two directions. So, this is what we need to do, Captain. Let me put emphasis on the being quiet. If we can do this quietly, we can turn the table on him."

"What do we do?" McClellan asked.

"I'll get O'Malley to get the men together and I'll explain my plan." He found O'Malley and then spoke with McClellan telling him his plan while O'Malley was gathering the men. In a couple minutes the men were gathered around Tye and McClellan.

"Listen, men." McClellan said quietly, barely above a whisper. "Tye thinks Tanza is going to hit us right at daybreak. Our plan is to turn the table on him and surprise him. Tye will take half of you and cover the ground to the east. Sergeant O'Malley and myself, with the rest of you, will cover the west. They will probably come in from two directions, and it will be quick. Have your rifle ready for the first shot. Don't try to reload, you won't have time. Have your pistol out and after firing your rifle, use it. It will be close in fighting. No talking, no smokes. Just be ready."

Tye took his six men to a small ditch that would offer some protection and McClellan did the same with eight men facing the opposite direction. The bedrolls were left as if someone was in them. The sentries were alerted and at the first sign of trouble, they would head to the ditch. It was going to be a long two hours or so waiting for something to happen.

~

Tanza had deployed his men, half would come in from the east and half coming in from the west. He was expecting to catch the bluecoats eating and drinking their coffee and still half asleep. About an hour before daybreak a light rain started falling, along with an occasional flash of lightning. The Apaches, expert at blending in with their surroundings, lay unseen by the sentries. When the signal came to attack, it would only be a forty or so yard sprint to reach the camp. Tanza figured most of the bluecoats would die in their bedrolls and if not, would get only one shot before they were overwhelmed by his warriors.

~

Even though all the troops were seasoned veterans, tension was high among the men in the ditch. No one liked waiting for a fight that lots of men were going to be killed. The minutes passed slowly as each man was deep in his own thoughts. Some prayed to God above to protect them and forgive them for their sins. Others thought of loved ones and wished they had paid a little more attention to them before they left on this patrol. Personal notes were being written by several to wives, girlfriends, or children. When the light rain started, it only added to the misery of waiting to die. All were sweating even in the coolness of the morning and the light rain that wasn't much more than a heavy mist.

Tye was calm, his mind working on the different possibilities of what might occur. He was sure the attack would come from the east with the sun being at the Apache's backs. He hoped he was right in that Tanza had split his band and would come from two directions at once. If he was wrong and they all came from one direction, the seven or eight guns that would be pointing in that direction would not do much good and they would be overrun quickly. He realized the light rain stopped as did the lightning and thunder. The only sound in the canyon was the occasional whinny of a horse and the stomping of their hooves. The clouds moved on and the sky in the east was turning gray with the approaching sun. It's time for men to live or die. Tye never felt more alive than at these moments.

McClellan was deep in his own thoughts. He had given specific instructions to the men that they would not fire till he and Tye told them to. If the Apaches did come from both directions at once there should be no more than twelve or fifteen coming from each direction. A volley from each side of the ditch should be devastating to them. At least that is what he was thinking. Under these circumstances, he was surprised he was as calm as he was. He looked over his shoulder to the east and saw the sun peeking over the rim of the hills. It was time.

◆ XVIII ◆

The serenity of the Texas sunrise was suddenly broken by a series of shrill Apache screams. The suddenness of the attack shocked every man, even Tye. Twenty- five screaming Apaches charging from two directions was loud enough to wake the dead and cause the men to want to find a hole and bury themselves. They were soldiers however, and most had saw this before. They stood their ground. The Apaches were darting in every direction, making difficult targets in the dim early morning light.

"FIRE." Came the command from Tye and McClellan almost at the same instant. The crashing sound of the volley of rifles only added to the tremendous noise. The jumpiness of the men caused most to miss their targets. Tye took one down with his rifle and grabbing his pistol, took another down. He saw two others go down and then it was total chaos in the ditch as Apaches dove on top on the men, striking with tomahawks and knives. Tye was on his back with his bowie stuck to the hilt in a brave's stomach. He ripped it upwards opening the mans belly like a gutted deer. The trooper to his left was dead, a tomahawk buried in his skull. The Apache was dead also as he was apparently shot by the soldier just as he struck with the tomahawk. The screams of both the soldiers and the Apaches combined with pistol shots was deafening. Tye shot a brave in the side of the head that was on top of McClellan. He then was hit from the side with what felt like a charging buffalo and knocked hard to the ground. The Apache was in mid air coming down on top of him when Tye struck up with his foot catching the Indian in the belly. Keeping his leg straight the brave's momentum resulted in him being thrown over Tye and hitting the ground hard on his back. He was up as was the Apache and they circled each other for just a couple seconds before the Apache charged with his knife coming up to rip into Tye's belly. Tye caught the mans wrist that held the knife and stopped its forward motion. The brave caught Tyes knife hand and held it in a vice like grip. They stood for a second chest to chest in what amounted to a draw. The Apache brought his knee up to catch Tye in the groin, but Tye, wise to that old trick, turned his hips making the knee strike him painfully on the side of the hip. Tye fell backwards pulling the brave with him and once again placing his foot in the Apache's stomach and throwing him in a somersault over his head. This time however, the Apaches head hit a rock and knocked him unconscious. Tye stood up breathing heavily and looked around to see hand-to- hand fighting everywhere. He pulled a brave off O'Malley that had stuck his knife in O'Malley's shoulder and from behind the Apache placing one arm across the warrior's chest and the other beside his head and with a violent shove, broke the Apaches neck, letting him fall limply to the ground.

Tye saw McClellan fighting like a madman, swinging his saber wildly. Two Apaches lay dead at his feet. Suddenly, it was over. Tye saw two or three Apaches running off. He looked around and saw the carnage… dead and wounded men, both red and white, were everywhere he looked. Troopers were sitting holding their heads in shock and exhaustion. A quick count showed six dead and almost everyone was wounded in one way or another. He counted eighteen Apaches in the ditch and five outside the ditch. Two of those in the ditch was still alive including the one he had knocked out. Enraged troopers found them and quickly killed them.

"You okay, Captain?" Tye asked when he walked over to where an exhausted McClellan sat on the ground.

"Guess so." He answered. "You?"

"Just a scratch or two. Nothing serious."

"Where's O'Malley?" McClellan asked as he stood up and for the first time looked around. "My God." A man could not hardly take a step that he didn't have to miss a body. "My God." He said again.

"O'Malley's fine. He has a knife wound in the shoulder, painful but not serious." I can't find Tanza among the dead. I saw two or three running off and one was probably him."

"We got all of them but two or three then?" McClellan said questionably.

"Yes Sir, but the big dog got away. He'll be pissed, Captain, and he's going to take his anger out on those captive children. I'm going after him and follow him to them. After that, I'll kill him."

McClellan looked around at the wounded soldiers. "Who are you taking with you."

"No one. I can move faster by myself and a hell of a lot quieter. Besides, you will need the ones that can ride to help you with the wounded. O'Malley can get you back to the Fort and he knows where a couple water holes are on the way. You'll be okay. Just give me some jerky and a couple canteens of water and I'm gone."

"Take what you need. And thanks from me and the men. We would have been caught sleeping if it wasn't for you." McClellan said shaking Tyes hand. "Good luck."

Tye gathered the canteens and jerky, saddled Sandy, and was gone. He looked back to see the men placing the dead Apaches in a pile. The dead soldiers were wrapped in blankets and tied to their horses. All the men besides McClellan, had a wound of some sort. A sorry looking lot." Tye thought to himself, then added. "Damn good fighting men though, every one of them." He turned back in the saddle and was gone, following Tanza tracks.

He found one of the Apaches where they had left their ponies. He was near death with a bullet in his belly. Reading sign, he saw where Tanza and one more brave had mounted their ponies and were racing as fast as they could go, due west and Mexico. "They are running those horses way too hard." Tye said to himself after about fifteen minutes of tracking. He held Sandy to a canter which he could hold for a long time.

~

About three miles ahead, Tanza was ignoring the pleas of his friend to slow down, that he was killing the horses. Tanza's blood was hot and he was thinking of nothing but those white and Mexican captives back at the river.

If nothing else, he would take his anger out on them. Five minutes later, he was brought back to reality when his horse floundered and dropped to his knees almost throwing Tanza. Tanza jumped off and with his knife slit the horse's throat. He grabbed his water gourd and took off running with the easy gait that the Apaches were known for and he would cover miles before tiring. The other brave was running with him.

~

Tye found the horses and knew that the tracking would get much harder now that they were on foot. Tye stood there thinking about the river. It dawned on him that there was only one crossing for several miles on the river and that had to be where Tanza was heading. Tye decided to gamble that was the place. He could make a lot better time not having to track them and with him being on horseback. He veered off the trail and struck a course that was shorter than the one Tanza was taking.

~

At the Apache's permanent camp on the Mexican side of the Rio Grande the captive children were being watched by two young Apache boys, neither over fifteen. Two women, Mexicans that had been captives for years, were also watching them. The children, five of them counting the two Turley children, were in good shape except for being a little hungry. They didn't know that pain and death was on its way toward them. The camp was a perfect hiding place. High cliffs were on three sides and the river on the other. The river here was deep and had a strong current making it impossible to cross. The only way into and out of the camp was a tunnel that was barely big enough for one horse at a time.

~

The gentle rolling hills that Tye had been riding thru was now giving way to a much different terrain. As he got closer to the river, it was going to get a lot rougher. It was almost dark now and Tye was letting Sandy pick his way. Horses had better eyesight than a man, especially after dark. After he stumbled a couple of times though, Tye decided to stop for the night. He unsaddled Sandy and brushed him down before giving him water and oats. Tye sat down and chewed jerky, washing it down with warm water from his canteen. He was dead tired from the fight and from the chase. He made sure Sandy was picketed and spread his bedroll close to him. He would depend on Sandy to give him a warning if anyone came close. He lay there looking at the stars and thought about his chances of winning the race to the crossing. Tanza was on foot but like he said before, that's not a big problem for a Apache. You put an Apache on foot and a white man on a horse for a fifty mile race, the Apache will win most of the time. Right now he figured he was a little closer than Tanza was to the river. He also figured Tanza had to put up some place for the night unless he wanted to risk a broken leg or worse.

He thought of Rebecca and how her body felt pressing against him and her tears the last time they were together. He closed his eyes and could see her beautiful face as he bent to kiss her lips. He could see her standing, waving good bye and probably wondering if he would be coming back. He wondered if it was right putting a woman thru that time and time again. In his line of work, he had already lasted longer than any other scout had at Clark. He knew six of them had been killed since he had been there. He decided it was something they needed to talk about. He could try something else to make a living but scouting was all he knew. Yeah, they had better talk about it.

~

It was pitch dark and Tanza was feeling his way more than seeing. It was dangerous and he was taking a chance but he had to get to the crossing before the army did. He knew Tye would be after him. He had shot at him during the fight and missed. He saw him standing when he and the other two had fled the fight. He also figured Tye knew that this was the only crossing for miles. It was a simple race to see who got there first.

His friend was moving beside him, but it was so dark he was only a shadow. When Tanza slipped and almost fell into a arroyo they decided to stop for the night. Drinking their water and eating pemmican they sat in silence reflecting on the day's events that had cost them so many friends." How do you think they knew we were coming?" Lone Wolf asked his friend.

"Watkins." Tanza answered. "Scout Watkins. I think he must be part Apache."

Lone Wolf just grunted his agreement and lay down on the still warm ground and went to sleep. Tanza, even though he was tired, found sleep hard to come to him. He was wound up tight and ready to explode. He finally slept but woke frequently, and would listen for any unnatural sound. He finally drifted off in a sound sleep. It was after dawn when he woke up and he was angry with himself. He woke Lone Wolf up and they immediately started toward the crossing.

~

Tye had been moving well before dawn, letting Sandy pick and choose his path. He was closer to the river than he thought as he saw a rock formation on a hill that he knew was close to the crossing. "We'll know in a few minutes, ole boy, if we won the race or not." He topped a hill and looked down on the crossing, seeing no one. He rode swiftly down the slope to the crossing keeping Sandy in the rocks to the side of where he figured the Apaches would come. He knew the first thing Tanza would do would be to check for tracks before exposing himself. Tye entered the swift but shallow water and walking along the bank on the Texas side checked for tracks. He saw none. He forded the river to the Mexican side and could find none there either. Elated he led Sandy downstream about thirty yards and out of the river on the Mexican side. He led him well into the brush and tied him securely to a large mesquite where he could not be seen. He found a place that was well hidden but still provided him full view of the crossing. He made himself comfortable, and waited.

He wasn't going to tip his hand until he saw which direction Tanza was going. He figured the camp was close but didn't know if it was up or down the river. He didn't wait long before he saw the two Apaches coming down the slope leading to the crossing. They were taking their time, looking carefully for any sign someone had been in front of them. Stopping at the river's edge they both looked carefully in all directions. Tye could feel their black eyes peering into the brush where he was. He was careful not to stare at them. Sometimes a fighting man can feel someone looking at them.

Satisfied they were alone, they started across the river. Tye slid farther back into the brush, waiting to see which way they went. Once across the river, they immediately headed upstream. They were no more than twenty yards from Tye, walking directly away from him. He stepped out of the brush and onto the sand by the river's edge. He had his pistol out and cocked. He followed them for eight or ten steps before they suddenly stopped. Tye stopped and was ready. Tanza slowly turned his head and looked over his shoulder at Tye. He said something and Lone Wolf moved to his left, away from him, then turned and looked at Tye. The Apaches were about ten feet apart now. Not a good situation for Tye. He knew that he could not take both down and he was probably going to take a hit. He just prayed it was not a fatal one. They all stood as statues for a moment then Lone Wolf raised his rifle to fire and Tye shot him square in the brisket and dove to his left at the same time causing Tanza's bullet to miss by inches. Tanza threw the rifle aside, shouting at Tye in Apache. Tye didn't understand all the words but he understood their meaning. His manhood was being challenged. Would he fight man to man or was he a old woman? Tye stood up and walked toward Tanza, stopping a few feet short of him. He holstered his pistol, loosened his gun belt pitched it to the side. Reaching down, never taking his eyes of Tanza, he pulled his Bowie out of the top of his boot.

A smile spread across Tanza's face when he realized his challenge had been accepted. He was full of confidence in his ability to take this white man even though he had heard about his prowess with a knife. He pulled his Bowie out of its scabbard and dropped into a crouch, his right hand holding the knife down low, edge up. Both men were on the balls of their feet, with their knees bent, ready to attack if the other left an opening. Both had his left arm a little out in front of their body to help with their balance and to ward off blows. Very few knife fights with two experienced fighters would end without both getting cut. They circled left to right, each feinting moves to see how the other would react. Tanza suddenly came forward and thrust his knife at Tye's groin. Tye was ready but still barely missed the razor sharp edge of the Apaches Bowie.

"Better be quicker than that old boy." Tye said to himself. "This is one quick Apache." Tye countered with a swipe at Tanza's neck. He missed the neck but left a shallow cut along Tanza's left shoulder. Tanza backed up a step and felt of the cut on his shoulder with his knife hand. He looked at the blood on his hand and at Tye with a look of hate that Tye would never forget. Never had Tye saw eyes that literally spit fire like Tanza's.

Tanza was not so sure of himself now...he had this thought before that this Watkins might be part Apache... now he was sure. Circling each other more, they move in closer to each other, knives out in front, moving back and forth, looking for the opportunity to strike. Tye suddenly grabbed Scar's knife hand just above the wrist with his left and struck upward with his own. He was suprised that his upward thrust was stopped and his hand felt as if it was in a vice. They now stood almost chest to chest, both holding the other's knife hand down and away in a standoff...it was now a test of who could hold on the longest.

Tye felt a shift in Tanza's body and knew the old trick of a knee in the groin was coming. He was ready for it and turned his hip, catching the knee in the side of his hip and it hurt like hell. Tye waited a second, his mind seeing the men, women, and children this murdering sonofabitch had killed, and he dropped a little lower and gathering himself, thrust himself up, chin on his chest catching Tanza flush in the face with the top of his head. Stunned by this blow Tanza's hand slipped off Tye's wrist. Tye thrust the knife into the man's stomach and pushing him back, let go of Tanza's knife hand. The Apache warrior stood there for a moment trying to stem the flow of blood and gore that was pouring the life out of him. He looked at Tye, dropped to his knees for a moment, then fell on his face and did not move. Tye wiped his knife on Tanza's breechcloth and walked over to Lone wolf to make sure he was dead.

He walked back to get Sandy and then retraced his steps to the two dead Apaches. He sat there for a moment trying to relax, trying to get the adrenalin out of his system. He reached for his makings in his shirt pocket and was surprise to see the blood that had soaked thru his shirt of the left side. With the fight, the adrenalin and everything else that comes into play at such a time, he hadn't realized he had been cut.

He forgot about rolling himself a smoke and dismounted and raised his shirt. It wasn't serious but it was a good four inch slice just above the belt. He knew it was going to be some bothersome before long. He walked to the river searching the shallow water and finally found what he was looking for...some moss. He made a wrap out of a shirt and after placing the moss on the cut, wrapped it with his shirt he had cut into strips. No the best medicine a man could have but maybe it will keep the infection down.

He remounted and started up river, looking for recent tracks or anything that might give him a clue as to where the camp may be. He came to a steep cliff that was going to make him swing way left, away from the river. He noticed that the cliff was continuing as far as he could see, away from where he figured the camp was. He was sure it was close and was on the river. He was searching for any sign, any indication that there was a way to get over this cliff which was probably fifty to sixty feet high and almost vertical.

He was almost back to the river when he saw it, a game trail heading toward the cliff. He dismounted and followed the trail. It led him to an opening of a tunnel. He walked in and could see light at the other end of the tunnel. "I'll be damned!" He exclaimed. "That has to lead to the camp." He walked back to get Sandy and took him into the tunnel with him. Stopping midway, he hobbled Sandy, an continued on foot. When he came to the end, he was looking at the Apache camp. He dropped to his stomach and scooted backwards a few feet staying in the darkness of the tunnel. He decided to wait and watch for awhile. Soon, two young Apaches came out of one the wickiups. They could not be more than fourteen or fifteen years old. As he watched, his heart stopped,. coming out of another wickiup was the Turley boy. Tears of joy ran down Tye's cheeks as he watch little Jim Jr. walk to the fire. "Thank you Lord." He muttered. "Thank you." Now where was little Marcy.

He did not want to kill the young bucks. He was trying to figure a way to get to the children without having to when a crazy idea hit him. It was so crazy that it just might work. Plenty of men had died already, he hoped no more did. He took Sandy back the way they had come and into the sunlight. He led him over to where Tanza lay. Picking up two large and fairly straight sticks he made a cross using strips of rawhide he cut from the sleeves of his buckskin shirt. He lifted Tanza onto Sandy and tied the cross he had made to his back holding him upright. He tied a rope to one foot and drew the rope under the Sandy's belly and tied the other end securely to his other foot. This would keep him from falling off Sandy, he hoped. Tye put a rope loosely around his own neck and led Sandy and Tanza back into the tunnel and out the other end into the camp. He walked with his hands behind him as if he was tied and being led by Tanza. Both boys jumped up when they saw Tanza and waved. From all appearances, Tanza had himself a white prisoner. They lowered their rifles and when Tye was close he pulled the pistol from behind him and got the drop on the boys. They were holding their rifles loosely at their side when Tye told them in Apache to throw them away. To Tye's relief, they did. He took their knives and tied their hands behind their backs. He cut the rope that held Tanza's feet together, and the body toppled off Sandy.

"Uncle Tye! Uncle Tye!" came a voice from behind him and he turned to see both Turley children running to him, throwing themselves into his arms. Tye held them tightly, tears of joy running unashamedly again down his cheeks. "It's over kids. Let's go home." He stood up and put them in the saddle, one behind the other.

"There is some other kids." Jim Jr. said. This caught Tye by surprise. Little Jim went back into the wickiup and appeared with four children, three of them Mexican and one white girl about seven or eight. Tye was worried now that with this many mouths, he would be short of food and water. He looked around the camp. He picked up some venison that was on the fire and wrapping it, put it into his saddle bag. He picked up two large gourds to hold water and gave one to Jim and the other, he carried. He spoke Apache to the women about not wanting any trouble.

"They are not Apaches uncle Tye." Jim said. "They are Mexicans and were captured a long time ago. Tye studied the women closely and could see they were Mexican. He asked them if they wanted to leave with them. One of them spoke telling him they had nothing to go back to...been to long ago since they had been captured. Tye understood and told them he appreciated how well they treated the children. One of the women brought him a bag of pemmican which was lean dry meat pounded into a powder and mixed with melted fat. It was a major food source of the Apaches. He thanked them again and left with the children and the two Apache boys. The boys hands were kept tied and a rope around their neck and tied to the pommel of the saddle on Sandy. Crossing the river, they filled all the gourds and Tyes two canteens.

"We will be a little hungry and thirsty before we get back to the Fort." Tye said to them. "Do not drink until we all do. It is three days back and we won't find a water hole till late tomorrow. Understand?" Each nodded their heads. They started the trek back with the kids alternating between riding and walking.

◆ XIX ◆

The patrol arrived at the Fort just before dark the second day after the battle. A large crowd of townspeople looked in horror at the bodies and the wounded soldiers. McClellan had sent a man ahead to report to Thurston on what happened. Word had filtered into town that the renegades had been whipped and Tye was after Tanza and the kids. Thurston and half the troops met the patrol at the bridge. Two army ambulances were there to put the more serious of the wounded in. Mrs. O'Malley was there as was Rebecca. Mrs. O'Malley ran to Sergeant O'Malley's side as did other wives and held their hands as the patrol crossed the bridge over Los Moras Creek and entered the Fort. Rebecca was with her. Thurston had already told her Tye was still out there. Thurston shook every mans hand as they came over the bridge. McClellan and he then went into his office. McClellan gave an accurate report of all the events including his stupidly chasing the Apaches. He could not say enough good things about Tye, much to Thurston's relief. Lt. Garrison was in the office and Thurston turned to him. Lieutenant, get three men and a couple of extra horses and head toward the crossing. He pointed to a spot on the map. See if you can find Tye."

"Sir, I would like to go also. I know where he should be." McClellan said.

Thurston took the cigar out of his mouth, a look of surprise on his face. "Hell man, you just got back. You look plumb wore out. "Yes sir, but I own that man and I want to help him if I can."

Thurston looked at him for a moment. "Bring another horse, Lieutenant. McClellan will accompany you."

They were on their way within fifteen minutes.

~

Tye was almost to the old mail road the second night after leaving the camp. He decided to stop and make camp at the spring he told them about. He couldn't remember when he had ever been so tired and his side was hurting something fierce. After eating the last of their food, Tye checked the Apache boy's hands to make sure they were not swelling. He tied their feet and then walked to where Sandy was picketed and lay down. Both Turley kids came over to him and lay down beside him, their arms laid across his chest. About midnight Sandy's snorting woke him up. He laid there for a moment listening. A minute later he heard the noise to. He knew immediately what it was and lifting the kids arms off him, stood up to meet the patrol. "Glad to see you, Garrison." Tye said as Garrison dismounted and hurried over to him.

"By God, you did it." He said as he saw the sleeping children and shook Tyes hand vigorously. The other three soldiers came over and shook Tyes hand.

"Never was a doubt was there." A familiar voice coming from the darkness said.

"McClellan. Is that you?" Tye hollered in disbelief.

"No one else." McClellan said as he came into the light of the fire.

"I figured you would have taken a hot bath, gotten drunk, and passed out by now."

"I knew how helpless you are out here so I figured I had better come to rescue you." McClellan said, bringing boisterous laughing from everyone.

"What about Tanza?" Garrison asked.

"Dead. Left him on the ground at the Apache rancheria where I found the kids."

"Corporal Tighe." Garrison said. "You head back to the Fort. Tell Thurston we will be in about mid morning. Tell him Tanza's dead and the children are safe."

"Yes sir." He mounted and left.

"I know ya'll want to chew the fat some but I'm bushed." Tye said. "I'm going back to sleep. See you gents in the morning."

Horses were picketed and all turned in except a sentry. You never let your guard down out here.

~

The whole town of Brackettville lined the Old Mail Road as the patrol came in with the kids. Guns were being fired into the air and townspeople were rushing to shake Tye's hand. When they crossed the bridge, the troops were lined up on both sides of the road leading to headquarters. Tye was looking past all this though. He was looking for someone else and when he saw her, all his tiredness left him. He dismounted and met her as she came running to him. A roar went up from the soldiers when they kissed. She looked at Tye and then past him, to the children. "Thank God all of you are safe." she tearfully whispered in his ear.

"We were real lucky to get them back. It was close, just a matter of a hour or so and Tanza would have killed them all."

Corporal Jensen cleared his throat to get Tye's attention. When Tye looked at him he said. "Major Thurston would like to see you in his office for a few minutes."

Tye looked at Rebecca. shrugged his shoulders and turned to leave. He looked back at her as he walked off." See you in a little while honey.'" He said.

"I'll be waiting." she said, then added. "Oh Tye, one more thing, take a bath and change your clothes." She made a face and held her nose as they both laughed.

"My God." she said noticing the bloody shirt for the first time. "You're hurt."

"Nothing to worry about." I'll get old sawbones to look at it." He kissed her again bringing more hoots and hollering from the men. "See you shortly."

Thurston greeted him as he entered the office. "Outstanding job, Tye. Simply outstanding."

"We lost a lot of men Major." Tye said accepting Thurston's handshake.

"I know that. I have McClellan's report. I hate as much as anyone, maybe more, to see men die, but that's the price of victory sometimes. You did a hell of job, Tye. Not only preventing more deaths by killing Tanza but by getting the children back. I don't know another man that could have done it."

"Thanks, Major. I do have a favor to ask though."

"Just you name it."

"The two young Apaches I brought in. Would you see to it they are not harmed. I would like to take them back to the reservation in the morning.

"Consider it done. I was going to go to the reservation in the morning to see the old chief. You can ride with us."

"Yes sir. Is that all, Sir?"

Thurston laughed. He knew Tye wanted to clean up and see Rebecca. "That's all. I'll see you early in the morning. Go to the hospital first and get that wound looked at."

"Yes Sir." Tye walked out on the porch and looked around.

"O'Malley took Sandy. Said you needed to clean up and take care of that pretty gal of yours." Lieutenant Garrison said and gave Tye a wink and laughed as he walked off. Tye headed to the hospital before going to clean up.

~

Tye arrived at the O'Malley's shortly before lunch.

"Figured you could smell a home cooked meal." Sergeant O'Malley said.

"How's the shoulder?" Tye asked referring to the knife wound O'Malley had received.

"Only hurts when my heart beats." O'Malley said with a half smile.

Tye laughed but knew the pain that a knife wound like than can cause. He had had a few of them in his life and had the scars to prove it. "Where's Rebecca?"

"Getting herself all fixed up for some damn old scout that's coming by."

"That old scout looks better than he did a hour or so ago." Rebecca said standing in the door of her room. She came over and gave Tye a quick kiss on the cheek. "Smells better too. It's a wonder what a little soap and water will do for a person, isn't it."

"I guess that means that after we're married you expect me to bathe more than once a week then." Tye said laughing.

"Only if you want to sleep with me." Rebecca said, then her face turned red when she realized what she had said.

Tye and O'Malley were bent over they were laughing so hard.

"If you two heathens can get control of yourselves, lunch is ready." Mrs. O'Malley said harshly.

"Settle down now, Momma. We're just having a little fun." O'Malley said.

Lunch was on the table. Lunch consisted of fried venison, gravy, potatoes, and corn. Tye was eating heartily. "First thing I've had to eat in a week besides biscuits and jerky." He said. " Sure is a fine meal, Mrs. O'Malley."

"You will be glad to know that Rebecca fixed it Tye."

Tye looked at Rebecca and said. "Really... beautiful and can cook too. How lucky can a man get, Sergeant?"

After lunch, Tye and Sergeant O'Malley sat on the porch while the ladies cleaned and washed the dishes. "You outdid your reputation on this patrol, Tye. People will remember you bringing those kids in for a long time. Speaking of the kids, what are they going to do?"

"I guess.. stay with me... I don't know for sure. I haven't had time to think about it much." Tye answered.

"Here's something to think about. Momma and me haven't had any kids around for a long time. We would love to have them stay with us...as family."

Tye looked at him. "Are you sure.?"

"We've talked about it, prayed about it. I think it would be a good thing for them, and it would fill a void in our lives."

Tye was shocked and happy all at the same time. "That sounds real good, Sergeant. We'll see how it works out."

The ladies came out on the porch. "Lets take a walk pa and let these two lovebirds have a moment to themselves." Mrs. O'Malley said. They left, and Rebecca came over and sat down beside Tye on the step of the porch. She put her head on his shoulder and placed her hand in his. "Its been a long week, Tye. Not a single minute of it went by that I didn't think of you, and worried about you."

Tye took his hand and turned her face up to his and kissed her. " I've missed you too. Each night, laying looking up at the stars I was thinking of you." Can't say it was every minute though cause I was busy trying to keep my hair some of the time." He said laughing.

"Tye, did Sergeant O'Malley say anything to you about them keeping the Turley children?"

"Just a few minutes ago, right before ya'll came out."

"What do you think about it.?"

"I am going to talk to the children. Personally, I think its great."

"Me too. They have a lot of love to give." Rebecca said.

The rest of the afternoon was spent holding hands, talking, and walking along the banks of Los Moras Creek. They were talking mainly of the wedding which Tye had promised when this last scout was over. It was almost sundown when Tye told her he had to get some rest. He told her he was going to the reservation in the morning and would see her when he got back. They stood on the porch, holding each other for a long time.

"One thing I thought of while lying in my bedroll one night was if I should put you thru this every time I go out."

"Put me through what?"

Tye looked her in the eyes. "I know that when I leave on patrol you have to wonder if I will come back or not. That's a lot to ask of any one."

She was quiet for a moment then answered. "Mrs. O'Malley and I have talked about that very thing. It's no different with you than with her or any other soldier's wife. She said if you love your man you can't let something like that stop you. When he's with you, love him and cherish him. That's what I'll do with you Tye. I love you more than anything in this world. Don't you know that?" She pulled him close and held his head against her breast. He felt her tears on the back of his neck. "I love you Tye Watkins." she sobbed.

He looked up, cupped her face in his large hands and kissed her. "I love you, Rebecca and don't you ever worry about me not coming back to you."

Walking back to his quarters, he stopped and looked up at the sky. "Jim, you and Marie can rest easy now. Your grandkids are safe and headed to a loving family. Rest in peace old friend. Rest in peace."

The old chief was standing outside his wickiup when they arrived. The two young bucks was released and Thurston told the story about the fate of Tanza and his band to the chief and some of the other older men of the tribe. They only nodded a few times as the interpreter repeated Thurston's words. The men remounted and turned to leave the rancheria. As they did, Tye felt eyes on him and he turned and looked back. Seeing nothing he shrugged, turned back and rode on with the others. Behind him, standing in front of his wickiup, twenty year old Grey Owl aimed an imaginary rifle at Tye's back and pulled the trigger. He smiled at the thought of him killing the great white warrior. ' I will... and soon,' he thought to himself.

◆ About the Author ◆

Border Trouble is Gary's first attempt at becoming an author. He has had a life long love affair with the Old West. This love could be traced back to his parents both of whom read westerns for years. He was amazed at the heroes, heroines, and villains of the Old West to life on the pages of their books. At the age of sixty-two he finally decided to try his hand at being a published author.

Gary was born in Levelland, Texas in 1943 and lived there until he was twenty years old. His mother, sister and several other relatives still live there. He was an athlete in High School earning a football scholarship at nearby Texas Tech University in Lubbock. He played there long enough to have two knee operations that ended his football career.

For the last thirty years he has lived in Odessa, Texas with his wife of twenty-five years, Debbie. They have four children, three boys and a girl. Like ninety percent of the other people in Odessa, his work is related to the oil field business and is proud to be part of what he laughingly calls "oil field trash."

Printed in the United States
43358LVS00001B/73-102